The adventures in this book are not all Doctor Dolittle's, and not all of them are set in Puddleby, but they are all to do with Doctor Dolittle and his animal friends, which is good enough.

Here you learn for the first time the amazing adventures of the shipwrecked sea dog, how Dapple the Dalmatian came to be the only pedigreed inhabitant of the Crossbred Dogs' Home, and what befell poor Gub-Gub in the Dog Ambulance, not to mention how Jip and Kling (the dog detectives) solve the mystery of the stunned man, how cleverly Doctor Dolittle himself saved the green-breasted martins of Africa from extinction, and what it is like to be a maggot who longs to travel.

This final collection of Hugh Lofting's stories was arranged in book form after his death by his sister-in-law, but it contains some of his most amusing and ingenious work.

And don't forget, if you want to read more Doctor Dolittle stories, all his other eleven adventures, from *The Story of Doctor Dolittle* to *Doctor Dolittle and the Green Canary*, are published in Puffins too.

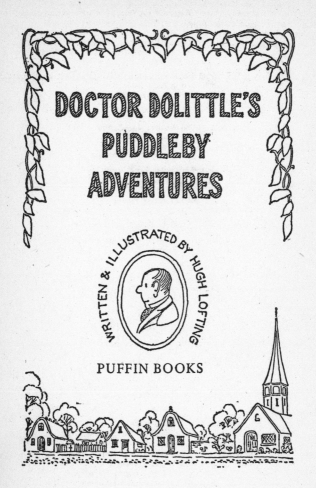

DOCTOR DOLITTLE'S PUDDLEBY ADVENTURES

WRITTEN & ILLUSTRATED BY HUGH LOFTING

PUFFIN BOOKS

Puffin Books, Penguin Books Ltd, Harmondsworth, Middlesex, England
Penguin Books, 625 Madison Avenue, New York, New York 10022, U.S.A.
Penguin Books Australia Ltd, Ringwood, Victoria, Australia
Penguin Books Canada Ltd, 2801 John Street, Markham, Ontario, Canada L3R 1B4
Penguin Books (N.Z.) Ltd, 182–190 Wairau Road, Auckland 10, New Zealand

—

First published by Jonathan Cape 1953
Published in Puffin Books 1969
Reprinted 1976, 1981

—

Copyright © The Estate of Hugh Lofting, 1953
All rights reserved

—

Made and printed in Great Britain by
Hazell Watson & Viney Ltd,
Aylesbury, Bucks
Set in Linotype Pilgrim

Except in the United States of America,
this book is sold subject to the condition
that it shall not, by way of trade or otherwise,
be lent, re-sold, hired out, or otherwise circulated
without the publisher's prior consent in any form of
binding or cover other than that in which it is
published and without a similar condition
including this condition being imposed
on the subsequent purchaser

CONTENTS

FOREWORD

THIS final selection of Hugh Lofting's animal stories and illustrations contains – in my opinion – some of the best of my husband's works. None of the stories has ever appeared in book form. I now offer them as being fully worthy to be included in this, the last of the Dolittle series.

The story of the Maggot was a favourite of my husband's and awaited the time when he thought it right to include it in a full-length Dolittle adventure. This he was not privileged to do, and I therefore am happy to be able to bring it – and others – to his admiring readers.

Because some of the stories were written in sequence with others, my sister, Olga Michael, has written a short introductory paragraph to these to clarify the settings and introduce the characters. Otherwise, they stand as originally written.

The chapter: DOCTOR DOLITTLE AND HIS FAMILY, which precedes the first story, is added for new readers with the hope that they, by beginning this book at that point, will come to know the good Doctor, his human friends, and all the lovable animals who played such an important part in the adventures of John Dolittle and his friends.

JOSEPHINE LOFTING

INTRODUCTION

DOCTOR DOLITTLE
AND HIS FAMILY

IN the beginning Doctor Dolittle was a people's doctor. He prescribed pills and tonics and mended broken bones the way regular doctors do. Besides working at the profession of doctoring sick people he also doctored animals. In the course of caring for his animal friends he acquired so many regular animal boarders in his house that there was barely room for a human patient to get in the front door. He had white mice in the piano, rabbits in the pantry, and a pig who slept in the vegetable bin. Even the linen closet was occupied by a family of squirrels.

When his human patients complained of the crowding and refused to come to him unless he got rid of the animals, Doctor Dolittle stopped doctoring humans entirely; he became an animal doctor only. Polynesia, the parrot who became a member of the Doctor's household, helped him change from a people's doctor to an animal doctor. She taught him to speak the language of the animals. Being a parrot, Polynesia could talk in two languages – people's language and animal language. She was able to explain to the Doctor the meanings of the nose-twitching, ear-scratching and tail-wagging signals that make up the language of animals.

'But, Polynesia,' said John Dolittle, 'birds don't have noses to twitch and ears to wag and – a – er – it's all too confusing.'

'Not at all, Doctor,' replied Polynesia. 'Birds speak a language all their own. Just listen to those nut-hatches on the window-ledge. Hear how they chatter and whistle and make clucking noises. The little fellow – the one with the dark markings on his wings – he's showing his friends the sights around Puddleby. He just told the other one that this is Doctor Dolittle's house.'

'My goodness! You don't say so!' said John Dolittle. 'Do let me write it down.' He rushed to his desk and brought out a notebook. 'Now tell it slowly,' he said as he scribbled away. 'I must get it all down so that I won't forget.'

It wasn't long before Doctor Dolittle was able, not only to understand what the animals were saying, but to speak their language as well. At first it was difficult because he had to learn to twitch his nose and scratch his ears as they did. The hardest part was the tail; he had to use his coat tails for that. The animals were amazed at the strange way the Doctor's coat tails flew around when he spoke to them. But very soon they became accustomed to it and understood him as well as they did their own animal friends.

Dab-Dab, the duck, was the Doctor's housekeeper. She cooked and scrubbed, dusted and cleaned, and went to market twice a week to keep the larder filled with assorted foods for the Doctor's strange family.

Gub-Gub, the pig, who also lived with the Doctor, fancied himself an authority on foods. He had a great curiosity that was always getting him into trouble.

The household accounts and the Doctor's business dealings were taken care of by Too-Too, the owl, who was a famous mathematician – among animals, of course.

Jip, the dog, had many duties. He organized and helped build and manage the Home for Crossbred Dogs which occupied a large part of the Doctor's garden. Whenever there was a job of scenting to be done, Jip had no equal. He could follow the trail of a man who was miles away simply by identifying the tobacco the man smoked.

When small objects – some as small as a pin – had to be found, Whitey, the white mouse, went to work. He had microscopic eyes and could even see the colours of a grain of dust.

Another member of the family was Chee-Chee, the monkey, who spent part of the time with the Doctor at Puddleby-on-the-Marsh and the other part in Africa where the climate was more to his liking. Whenever the Doctor went on a voyage he always sent for Chee-Chee to act as guide in following hidden trails and paths through jungles and foreign lands. He would climb the highest trees and swing along from limb to limb through the tangle of branches, calling out to the Doctor and his party the way the paths led.

Among the Doctor's animal friends who lived at Puddleby a good deal of the time, was a two-headed animal called a pushmi-pullyu. He had a head at each end of his body and could eat with one while talking with the other. The pushmi-pullyu said this enabled him to avoid talking with his mouth full.

Cheapside, the London sparrow who made his home in the ear of a statue on St Paul's Cathedral in London where he could see everything and know everyone who passed through the great city, was perhaps the most versatile of the Doctor's friends. John Dolittle often called on him for information about the movements of ships and people, and Cheapside never failed to find the answers.

Early in his career as an animal doctor, John Dolittle took into his home a young boy by the name of Tommy Stubbins. Tommy, as the Doctor's chief assistant, learned to speak the language of animals and helped Doctor Dolittle with their care. Because the Doctor was a busy man it was Tommy Stubbins who wrote down the adventures of the great doctor and his animal friends.

In the little town of Puddleby-on-the-Marsh, where the Doctor and his family lived, Matthew Mugg, the Cat's-Meat-Man, sold food for animals. Naturally he came to be a great friend of the Doctor and Tommy and often assisted them in their problems with the animals.

There were others who lived with the Doctor for short periods: Kling, the Dog Detective, Dapple, the prize Dalmatian, Toby and Swizzle, the circus dogs, and Bumpo, the African Prince – son of the king of Jolliginki.

The stories which follow in this book were written by Tommy Stubbins about the Doctor and his animal friends.

OLGA MICHAEL

THE SEA DOG

I

THE 'SEA SWALLOW'

THE Home for Crossbred Dogs was one of the most popular clubs in Doctor Dolittle's zoo. This was an institution which Jip, the Doctor's dog, had persuaded John Dolittle to establish for mongrel dogs who were left to wander the countryside without proper places to sleep or sufficient food to keep their ribs from showing.

Very soon after the Doctor's return to Puddleby-on-the-Marsh, kennels were built at the lower end of the garden for dogs who preferred private quarters. And one large house was added for those who liked to spend their time with company. The large house was also used as a sort of club room.

It was to this club that the Doctor and I, Tommy Stubbins, went one evening on our regular tour of inspection. As we entered the building we were astonished at the quiet, for usually, even during meals, the Home for Crossbred Dogs was a pretty noisy place. Proceeding to the dining room we found the explanation for the stillness: an after-dinner story was being told by one of the members. The entire company was paying rapt attention, and but for the voice of the speaker not a sound could be heard.

The Doctor did not like to interrupt. He was always most particular not to interfere with the liberties of the various clubs in his zoo. He quietly sat down to wait till the story should be over, and I followed his example. Very soon we were both as deeply interested in the story as any of the audience.

The speaker was a rugged, thick-set sort of collie mongrel. Neither the Doctor nor I knew very much about him beyond the fact that he was one of the earliest applicants for membership when the club was first opened. His most important reason then for joining was that he could never settle down under private ownership. There wasn't liberty enough, he said. Now it appeared that he had spent a good deal of his life at sea. We learned afterwards from Jip that he was known among the members as the Sea Dog, and was one of the best story-tellers they had.

'This ship,' he was saying, 'was a nice enough ship – so was the crew, for that matter. But the Captain, well, the Captain was peculiar. Full of discipline, you know. And the trouble was that he felt that everything on his ship had got to come under his old rules and regulations – not only the crew, but dogs as well. I do believe that skipper would have made the very rats in the hold toe the line and keep a watch if he could. And of course that didn't suit me. I had always been as free as the air and on most ships I'd sailed with I had been given all the liberty I wanted. You might wonder why I stayed on this one – the *Sea Swallow* she was called. Well, I often wondered myself. At many a port I'd go ashore, saying, "Now that's the end. I'll not go back. Finish." But sure enough, when the hour for sailing came, I'd find myself dawdling down to the wharf just in time to catch her before she let go her moorings. Why, I couldn't tell you. But in spite of old Captain Burton and his strictness I stuck with the *Sea Swallow* for over two years. And if she hadn't got wrecked maybe I'd be with her still. And the curious thing is that I was the one who caused her wrecking – though I didn't mean to. And how it came about is the yarn I'm going to tell you tonight.'

At this a slight rustle of movement ran through the audience as the dogs settled down or sought new places where they could listen more comfortably. A few of the smaller dogs in the front rows looked round and, seeing John Dolittle at the back of the room, whispered to one another proudly that he had joined the audience.

'Captain Burton,' the Sea Dog went on, 'didn't believe in having anything loose around his ship. Everything had to be fastened up – dogs included. And whenever he saw me about the decks he'd always call for one of the men and tell him to lock me up in the carpenter's shop. The carpenter's shop was right up for'ard in the fo'castle. It was one of the dullest, most uninteresting places in the whole ship. And after I had spent an awful lot of time imprisoned there I began trying to think out some way of escape. It had two portholes, and I found I could reach one of them by jumping up on to the carpenter's bench. Outside there was nothing visible but the sea rushing aft and a gull or two sailing around. It occurred to me as I peered through, why shouldn't I just hop into the sea and get back on to the open decks of the ship further aft?

'Well, I wasn't a very experienced sea dog then or, of course, I would never have even dreamed of such a thing. But I was that bored with the stuffy old carpenter's shop I imagine I wasn't thinking of anything beyond getting out. Presently I heard four bells ring. That told me it was two in the afternoon. I calculated that if I waited till half-past two the Captain would then be taking his after-lunch nap, and maybe I could enjoy two or three hours' liberty before he spotted me and had me locked up again. So I sat on the carpenter's bench looking at the sea flying past, till I heard five bells. Then I just leaped through the porthole as though it had been no more than a hole in a fence.

'It's a wonder I'm alive to tell the tale. I was always a good swimmer, and plunging down into the rushing sea didn't bother me at all. But when I came up, shaking the water out of my eyes, and began to look at the side of the ship slipping by me at nine knots I saw not a thing that I

could cling on to – let alone climb up. I've often wondered since just how I expected to be able to climb back on to the ship. I suppose I had some notion there would be a rope ladder hanging down, or something of the sort. But even if there were, it is very doubtful if it would have saved me. Anyway, as the tail end of the ship slipped up to me and then past I thought, "Well, that's the end of you, you blockhead! You're free, all right. But now, unless you can find yourself an island to get on to, it's going to be a short life and a wet one."

'But I wasn't destined for a watery grave. On the stern rail of the ship as it went gliding by, one of the cabin-boys was leaning. Luckily he was looking down into the water – dreaming of home, I suppose, or something. And presently he sees my head go bobbing by in the foam of the wake.

' "Jiminy !" says he. "There's old Rover fallen overboard."

'And quick as a flash he grabs up a coil of light rope and heaves it out astern with a mighty nice aim. The tail end of it fell right across my face, which by this time was a good thirty yards behind the ship.

' "Good dog !" he calls. "Grab it, Rover, grab it !"

'And grab it I did – in my teeth. The salt water gurgled into my throat, but I managed to blow it out again, like a whale, without letting go. Then very gently Snooky – that was the cabin-boy's name – began hauling in on the rope. The drag of the rushing sea was fierce. But he kept an upward lift on the line so as to prevent the water from filling me up. And presently he had me alongside the ship, where the pull of the water was stronger than ever.

' "Now," says he, "hold on like death !"

'I took an extra grim bite on the rope and he began lifting me, like a fish on the end of a line, bodily out of the water. In mid-air I span till I was dizzy, but I didn't let go. And soon he had me over the rail and standing beside him on the deck.

'I tried to show him I was grateful. At first he had no idea of how I came to be floating in the sea. He supposed I had been kicked off the ship by the Captain or the bo'sun. But when he came to look into the matter he found that I had been locked in the carpenter's shop. And that the only way I could have got out, since the door was still locked, was through the porthole – also, because there was no one in the shop beside myself, I must have jumped out. That set him thinking.

'Snooky, the cabin-boy, had had to put up with a good deal of kicking and cuffing himself from the "Old Man", as we called the Captain. And this made him extra sympa-

thetic with me. He thought that any dog who would just jump into the sea to gain his liberty must be a pretty brave animal. He didn't know I was just a plain fool, but that's neither here nor there.

'"All right, Rover," says he. 'I'll keep your secret – anyway as long as I can. You've been drowned, you understand – jumped into the sea and went right down to Davy Jones's locker, bless you! Ship's carpenter will unlock the shop around seven bells, and he'll find you gone and the port open. So, of course, you must be drowned. In the meantime, I'll stow you away in the hold or a locker or something, and when no one's around I'll give you a run. And

I'll see you get three square meals a day. They don't know how to treat a dog aboard this ship – nor a cabin-boy, neither. But use your sense now, Rover, if you want to stay free. Lie low – like a drowned dog should. You're dead and buried, remember that." '

2

THE DOG HERO

'I T was a curious thing,' the Sea Dog went on, 'to find myself far freer in many ways after I was dead than I had been before. The cabin-boy Snooky was as good as his word. How he managed it without taking any of the ship's company into his confidence, I've no idea. But somehow he kept me hidden on that craft and not a soul knew. One day he would stow me in the hold where I'd lie on a sack among barrels and packing-cases; another, he'd shift me in a great hurry, secretly, to one of the store lockers where ropes and spare gear were kept. You see, on big ships there are many places which only get visited once in a long while in the course of a voyage. And the cabin-boy made it his business to find out as far as possible ahead of time when these places were likely to be opened.

'But the most wonderful part of all was how he took me out for runs – mostly after dark, of course. There wasn't a day passed that he didn't somehow give me a bit of exercise. There's no doubt that he knew the habits of all of the crew by heart, hour for hour. Just the same, it is quite a feat; not only to keep a dog's presence on a ship a secret, but to give him exercise into the bargain. And he managed to bring me food as well. It wasn't always enough – I strongly suspect that he often went without, himself, in order to feed me – but I was able to survive on it all right.

'And then I found that besides winning a new kind of freedom I had suddenly become a hero, too. I fancy that often happens to folks after they are dead. The Captain remarked one day:

' "What has happened to that dog? I haven't seen him around lately."

' "He has been drowned, sir," said the First Mate.

' "Drowned!" cried the Captain. "How was that?"

' "You had him shut in the carpenter's shop, sir," replied the mate. "When the carpenter went in there the door was locked as usual, the port open and the dog gone. Must have jumped into the sea, sir. Hasn't been seen since."

'This upset the Captain quite a little – and it upset the crew a good deal more. They had been fond of me and, in their rough way, kind. Sailors, you know, are a very superstitious lot. My death, when it became known, was taken as a most unlucky sign. Often when I was in hiding I'd overhear them talking about me. All my faults had been forgotten: only my good qualities were remembered – after my death. I decided I was a pretty fine dog. I even wept a little over my own sad end as I listened to them.

' "After all," said one, "a ship's dog is a mascot. The Old Man didn't treat him right. That's why he jumped into the sea. Poor old Rover! I remember well the first voyage he sailed with us."

' "Aye," said another. "It's a bad sign, the worst possible sign of ill luck, when a ship's dog dies at sea. I wish I hadn't signed on this voyage."

'About three days after my disappearance everybody aboard was talking about me. My sad and untimely death had cast a gloom over the whole ship. And the Old Man, although he was captain and boss of the roost, was in high disgrace. The crew didn't openly mutiny or show disrespect, of course. But in many little ways they managed to make him feel that it was his harsh treatment of me that had

caused me to jump through the porthole, and that whatever bad luck followed would be his fault.

'And then – quite unintentionally – I made matters much
worse myself. This way: One evening I was dreadfully
hungry. I knew food wouldn't be served till four bells – in
the dog watch. I peeped out of the deck-house cupboard
where Snooky had hidden me. Oh, I was so hungry! There
was no one about and darkness was coming on. The
fo'castle bell wasn't more than ten feet away. I nipped out,
took the rope of the bell in my teeth and rang it: *Dong,
dong* – *Dong, dong,* four bells! Probably the first time that
the dog-watch bells were ever rung by a dog.

'Well, all I had meant to do was to hurry up the cook with grub. But what I actually did was to throw the whole ship into something like a panic. I dashed back to my hiding-place and pulled the door to behind me. But through the crack I could see what happened. First, men came running up on deck from below, down from the bridge, from every corner of the ship.

' "Who rang that bell?" bawled the officer of the watch.

'The bo'sun promptly set to work to find out. He questioned every man and boy of the crew. All denied it. Finally they dispersed. Well, I was still hungry. I slipped out and rang the bell again. This time the bo'sun had the whole crew with him below – except the quartermaster at the wheel – and he knew none of his men *could* have rung it. When he came rushing back on deck he looked strangely pale and scared. So did many of the men. They examined the bell in silence. There was no means in evidence by which it could have been rung accidentally. Finally one old salt grunted out in a hoarse, frightened sort of whisper:

' "It's old Cruikshank all right. Gee! I wish I hadn't sailed in this craft!"

' "What does he mean – *old Cruikshank*?" I heard a cabin-boy ask of one of the deck-hands.

' "Why, John Cruikshank, the pirate," said the deck-hand. "We are passing over where he was drowned right now. And on any vessel that is doomed to go down old Cruikshank's ghost rings the ship's bell as it goes over his grave. Every sailor knows that. I reckon this is this boat's last voyage all right. Keep your life-preserver handy when you climb into your bunk tonight. That's all."

'From that moment,' the Sea Dog continued, 'things aboard the *Sea Swallow* began to go wrong. Sailors are strange folk. Of course they were more superstitious in those days than they are now. Many of the little happenings were nothing more than the natural mishaps of everyday life aboard ship. But the crew couldn't see that. My disappearance had been a bad enough sign; but when the ship's bell began ringing itself as we passed the latitude of Cruikshank's grave, then everything that happened after that was, for them, merely part of the chapter of accidents through which the *Sea Swallow* was sailing to her watery doom.

'I never saw men get so irritable and jumpy in my life. To make matters worse, one or two serious things happened as well. Sickness broke out on board. Several men had to keep to their bunks. Next, a seaman who had gone aloft to attend to the rigging fell and hurt his leg so badly that he had to join the sick list too. Then bad weather came along just as the skipper was short-handed. Quite a storm blew up and shoved the ship away off her course. Following that, came a long spell of fog, when they couldn't see the sun to take their bearings by and find out where they were.

'All of this the crew blamed on the Captain for his ill-treatment of me, which had caused my disappearance and brought on the bad luck. Very soon the men, with overwork and general jumpiness, reached a state bordering on mutiny. Then one night when I was going for a little quiet stroll I was seen by one of the deck-hands who let out a howl and ran up on to the bridge.

'"I seen the ghost of the dog, Captain," he stuttered through chattering teeth – "old Rover, sure as I'm alive I met 'im walking on the deck."

'As there was a fog on, the Captain was taking the wheel himself. At first he wouldn't believe it. But the man swore it was true and offered to take him and show him. The Skipper called to the quartermaster near him on the bridge to take the wheel. Then he followed the scared deck-hand down the companion ladder. In the dark he didn't notice that the quartermaster, worn out with doing double duty, had fallen fast asleep standing bolt upright.

'Hearing the Captain and the deck-hand coming down to look for me, I sped along up for'ard as far as I could go. I thought I would have the peak to myself. I had forgotten all about the lookout. I nearly scared him to death. At the first glimpse of me he left his post, and ran yelling towards the bridge. It seemed I had roused the whole ship and must be caught for certain. But just at that moment there was a dull thud and the ship came to a complete standstill, listing to starboard. Everything that wasn't fastened down slid along the decks for yards – including me.

'In the fog, with no lookout and no one in charge of the bridge, we had run aground.

'For the first time since I had been fished out of the water by Snooky I began to get scared myself. The lurch of the ship as she keeled over to starboard swung my door to with a bang. And there I was, shut in a closet with the ship going down maybe, and no way of getting out or of telling what was happening.

'Then I thought to myself, "Well, Snooky knows where I am. He won't get off the ship without me.

' "But what if Snooky should be killed – or kept so busy by the bo'sun that he couldn't come for me? In any case of course he would get in an awful row when he let on that he had been hiding me. Might he be afraid to own up and just go off and leave me?"

'All these thoughts flitted through my mind as I sat there in the darkness of the closet and listened to the men shouting and running about on the decks outside. Presently, to my great joy, Snooky dashed in, just to comfort me, not to take me out yet. It seemed the Skipper had hopes of saving the ship. We had run on to a sandbar or something. And with the sea calm the way it was this might be possible.

'Almost immediately Snooky dashed away again, trying to close the door after him lest the bo'sun should see me.

But I shoved my nose out so he couldn't close it. And he saw what I meant.

'"All right, Rover," said he. "I'll leave it ajar. Then if I can't come for you you'll be able to swim for it anyway."

'And it was lucky for me – and him – that he did. The Captain's efforts to get the ship off not only did not accomplish anything, but they wasted much valuable time that should have been spent in preparing to abandon the ship. The bank we had run on to turned out to be part sand and part rock. I am not sure that the Skipper suspected the ship had torn a hole in herself, but certainly he had no idea how large a one. Presently, with the filling of the hold with water the ship gave a terrific lurch from starboard to port. She lay over so far the decks were half under water and too steep for anything but a fly to walk on.

'I heard yells and cries all over the ship. Many of the men I imagined had been hurled into the sea by the sudden lurch. And I knew from the list on her that all the lifeboats on one side must be useless.

'Something told me that the serious moment had come and that I had better get out into the open without delay. I flung the door open with all my weight and scrambled out on to the crazily sloping decks.'

3

THE END OF THE 'SEA SWALLOW'

'AND I was only just in time.

'"Look out!" yelled a voice from the darkness near by. "She's going down!"

'Suddenly I felt the ship sliding back off the bar. She righted herself as she slid. But she went on settling fast and then began to tip, stern down, bow up. In the darkness I couldn't see much, but I knew it was the end. Soon the decks were rearing up skywards like the side of a house. I didn't want to slide down on to the top of the tangled gear. The sea was rushing and gurgling into the aft portholes with a terrible noise. I hopped up on to a pile of hawser and leapt clear over the rail into the sea.

'My one idea at first was to get off, away from her, far enough to be clear of the wash when she disappeared. I had no notion then what we had struck, whether there was land near or not. As I said, with the stillness of the night, the sea was pretty calm – luckily. I struck out away from her, but also somewhat towards the direction she had been travelling in. It was here, I thought, if there was land at all, that I would find it.

'On the way I heard and saw several of the crew swimming near me. It looked as though none of the lifeboats had got away at all. I wondered what had happened to poor Snooky. After swimming another ten minutes I stopped and listened. Away off to my right I thought I heard through the fog the sound of breakers. If it was, that meant land of some kind. I was in good form and I reckoned I could go on swimming like this for another half-hour yet. Turning my nose in that direction I ploughed ahead.

'I hadn't gone very far before I heard a great splashing near me. At first I was scared – of sharks. But on second thought I told myself that no shark ever made a racket like that and they were almost unknown in these waters anyway. Then I heard a voice, Snooky's voice, gasping and calling through the fog for help. I turned again and spurted off at my best speed towards the voice.

'When I found him I saw at once that Snooky was in a bad way, exhausted and as feeble as a child.

' "I'm done for, Rover," he groaned – "Wind. ... My wind's all gone."

'Well, I was just distracted. He had saved my life from the sea. Never had I wanted anything so much as I wanted to help him. But I saw instantly that I could do nothing till I had made sure about this land which I hoped to find off to my left there behind the veil of fog. Before I left him I tried to make him understand I was just going to look for land and coming back. But of course I couldn't.

'I was glad that the darkness hid his face from me as I turned and left him gasping and floundering alone.

'I knew of course,' the Sea Dog continued, after pausing a moment to take a lap or two from a water-bowl that stood near, 'that if I didn't get back to Snooky soon he wouldn't be there any more. I never swam so hard in my life.

'Presently I thought I could catch the whiff of land through the dampness of the fog. It was a great night for smelling. I put on still more speed. The murmur of breakers or whatever it was – sounded clearer. Now I felt pretty certain there was land ahead. How far? That was the question. Soon the water began to grow frothy and foamy around me. ... And then – oh, it was a wonderful moment, I can tell you! My feet touched bottom! I scampered up a flatly sloping beach. It was very little I could see through the darkness and the mist. But it *was* land: that was the important thing. I turned, and making as sure of my bearing as I could, plunged back into the water in the direction I had come from.

'I hoped Snooky would still be splashing or calling. If he wasn't I would have hard work finding him. After I had swum what I calculated was about the distance I had come, I stopped and listened again. All was still. My heart grew cold. Was I too late then? ... But what was that? I held my breath. The night was as still as a church. ... Yes, it was a groan – a little way ahead. Frantically I ploughed on. And presently I ran right into him. He seemed more dead than alive but his chin was still above water. I wondered if he would have sense enough to do what I wanted him to do. I took his coat-sleeve in my teeth and shook him. He opened his eyes and seeing me seemed to give him courage. He grabbed hold of my coat between the shoulders and I started off. All I wanted him to do now was to float. So long as he didn't throw his arms about me I could do the rest.

'It was heavy work and I had to go slow. With a freight like him in tow, I had to nurse my wind. But the calm weather was in my favour and, luckily, Snooky had sense enough to see what I was trying to do and to help me. He could still just keep his chin up, lying flat, but he hadn't wind or strength enough to swim another stroke. Yard by

yard, as I towed him along, I heard that surf-roar coming nearer through the fog. Presently he heard it too and managed to gasp out:

'"Good dog, Rover! You'll do it yet. Good old dog! Land ahead!"

'When at last he felt the sand bumping his feet beneath the water, new life seemed to come into his exhausted body. And with me beside him he staggered up the beach through the darkness – then fell among the stones of the shingle in a dead faint. As he fell a little wind came whispering off the land. I lay down beside him breathing and blowing like a grampus. . . .'

Much earlier in the course of the Sea Dog's story I had noticed Jip come into the hall. With a nod of approval he had settled down near us to listen. I could well understand that the speaker was popular with the club members as a spinner of yarns. The Home for Crossbred Dogs was by no means an easy audience to address – as I knew from experience. Yet this evening the large gathering, from the beginning of the story to the end, never stirred, not even when the Sea Dog paused to moisten his throat at the water-bowl. Every listener, silent, wide-eyed, with ears cocked, waited for him to go on.

'The next day,' he continued after a moment, 'I awoke to find the sun shining brightly down upon a pleasant island. Poor Snooky was still fast, fast asleep. Without waking him, I rose and trotted along the beach to explore a bit.

'The first thing I noticed was the masts of our stranded ship sticking up out of the sea. The shelf or bar, or whatever it was she had come to grief on, was apparently wide enough to keep part of her above water still. But she was ruined – anyone could see that. And the next rough sea that came along would certainly beat her to pieces in no time. She lay out from the land about three-quarters of a mile. I found various members of the crew, all fast asleep, scattered along the beach. From the slant of the sun I reckoned it was about five o'clock in the morning.

'Then I wandered inland into the hills of the island. It wasn't tropical exactly – sort of half tropical. The climate was good. I smelt deer and rabbits everywhere. I decided we might have fared much worse. Next, I smelt the scent of a man. I followed it and came upon the Captain – also fast asleep.

'The sight of him made me think that maybe I had better go and wake Snooky before I did any more. So I went back to the beach and pulled him gently by the sleeve.

'He woke with a start and I managed to convey to him that I wanted him to follow me. I took him to where the Captain lay. And, as I had expected, he was not at all anxious to awaken him. He was still scared of what might happen if it became known that he had hidden me. Then I led him away into the higher parts of the island. And I started to look for water. I followed a deer-track and it led me, as I hoped it would, to a drinking hole – a beautiful rocky hollow in the hills where a sparkling stream leapt in at one end and trickled out at the other. At sight of it poor Snooky gave a cry of joy, flopped down and took a drink. So did I – for I was as thirsty as a red herring.

'After we had had a drink and a wash I caught a rabbit. We hadn't any matches to light a fire, so we had to eat it raw. Then we both felt better. Snooky took off his clothes and hung them on a bush to dry. After that we set about making some sort of a shelter in which to live.

'Late in the day we heard sounds from the beach where the rest of the crew had woken up and were stirring about. I thought maybe we had better keep an eye on them. So I led Snooky quietly down the hillside, where we presently found a flat rock jutting out through the foliage, from which we got an elegant view of the beach and all that was going on.

'The men, under the direction of the Captain and bo'sun, were trying to save things off the old ship before the sea broke her up. Some of the best swimmers had swum out to her and had got one of the lifeboats free from the tangled gear. In this they were now plying backwards and forwards between the beach and the ship bringing stores ashore.

'About noon Snooky and I saw smoke rising from down below. So we knew that the crew had succeeded in finding some matches still dry. And a little later smells of food cooking made both our mouths water as the wind swept the odour upwards towards our hillside lookout. By the time the second night had come on I knew that poor Snooky was pretty lonely for human company – and human food. Of course he had me. But that's the way humans are : one man is company enough for a dog, but one dog isn't company enough for a man – at least not for long.

'The cabin-boy was still afraid of the anger of the Captain if he should find out that he had been hiding me on the ship when everyone thought that I was drowned. And, though he often sneaked down within earshot of the crowd on the beach, he never showed himself. And, of course, they, no doubt, supposed that he'd been drowned.

'After a while I decided that there was no reason why we shouldn't share some of the luxuries that the crew were enjoying. And while Snooky was asleep one night I slipped down to the beach and did a little reconnoitring. I waited in hiding till the conversation round the beach fire had died away, and I was sure that all the men were asleep. Then I sneaked up to where I knew the stores were kept – under a shelter of boughs and tarpaulins.

'I have to smile every time I think of that night, for before day broke I had made several trips up and down the mountain. And when Snooky awoke the next day he found beside his bed of leaves an elegant piece of corned beef, a loaf of bread, a tin of sugar and half a Gloucester cheese – the first real food besides raw rabbit he had seen in four days. Also – a very important item – I had brought a box of dry matches.'

4

ROVER DISAPPEARS

'ALAS! Poor old Snooky got lonesomer and lonesomer. He was just dying to go down and join that crowd on the beach. And still he hadn't quite the courage to face the Captain. If I had known how to, I believe I would have told him to go without me and let me stay in the wilds of the island. I felt sure I could pick up a living all right, for a while anyhow, with the rabbits and the fresh-water brook and the rest. It would have been lonesome for me, of course, I knew that. But dogs can stand lonesomeness better than men can. And, anyway, I would have willingly done it for him who had saved my life and done so much for me.

'But the trouble was, of course, I *couldn't* tell him. I

could make him understand simple things – by signs and so forth – but that was too hard. Then I said to myself, I said,

' "Now, Rover, my boy, you're standing in this lad's way. If you weren't here he would have no cause to fear the Skipper, and he could go right down and join the crew and be happy. Suppose they sail away without him some time and he perishes on this island alone. It will be your fault – Rover, my boy, *you've got to disappear*."

'This idea of the crew sailing away without him had bothered Snooky, too, I knew. All day and every day – pretty near – he'd lie hidden in the bushes watching the crowd on the beach below. They had rigged up a flag mast, hoping passing ships might see it and come to the rescue. As I watched him watching them, it became quite clear to me that he was terrified that any day they might grow tired of waiting to be rescued and would put to sea in the lifeboats and leave him behind.

'That evening he says to me, he says – he liked to talk, you know, even though he supposed that I couldn't understand – "Rover," says he, "I'll go down tonight. The worst the Skipper can do is give me a licking. I'm sick of being alone. I'll go and face him tonight."

'And when darkness had come he made his way down towards the bright fire on the beach. He sneaked up quietly – to see how the land lay. As it happened, the Captain was just haranguing one of the crew for something he'd done wrong. Sparks seemed to be flashing from the Skipper's eyes. He surely could look terrible, could Captain Burton, when he was mad. And tonight he was madder than we had ever seen him. ... Well, poor Snooky lost his nerve once more and crept back again up the hill.

' "I'll do it tomorrow, Rover," says he, as he lay down to sleep. "I'll really do it tomorrow – if I don't, maybe they'll sail without me and then I *will* be in the soup. As sure as

I'm alive, I'll go down and face the Captain tomorrow. And you'll come with me, Rover. We may get it hot. But it will be better than this. I'm sick of being alone."

'Well, I was afraid that when the morning came he would lose his nerve again. So that night I determined I would just disappear, in order that he need have no further cause to fear the Skipper.

'About midnight, when he was snoring away like a bear, I gave him one last look and hit the trail. It was a biggish island, a good ten miles long and two or three wide. I wandered off towards the other end of it, away from the beach and the crew. I must confess I felt very miserable at leaving him, but at all events I had the satisfaction of knowing that I was doing the right thing.

'When morning came I heard him running through the woods calling and searching for me.

' "Rover, Rover, where are you?"

'But I just lay low, knowing that after a while he'd give up and go down to join the crew. He didn't give up in a hurry, though. Plucky boy, he didn't want me to be left behind. All that day I heard him, off and on, at different parts of the island, trying to find me. But when evening started to come on I heard him no more and I knew he had gone to the beach.

'That night was a very wretched night for me. I kept telling myself that sooner or later a ship would come to get water or something and would take me off the island. But I didn't succeed in cheering myself up much. We dogs miss human company pretty badly when we have grown up with it, and I had become very, very fond of Snooky, the cabin-boy.

'When the dawn came the island seemed strangely silent. I thought I'd go down to the other end and spy around a little to see if he had really joined the crew. So very quietly I made my way along through the underbrush. I came to

Snooky's old camp. He wasn't there. "Well," I thought, "he has gone, then. Good luck to him!"

'I went on down to the lookout rock and scanned the beach. The boats were gone too – and the crew. Of course it was what I had expected, planned, to be left alone on the island thus for his sake. But when I looked down at the empty beach and realized that they were *all* gone, that the thing was done, never to be undone, it was a great shock. I was sort of stunned by it. It was all very well to tell myself that a ship would come, but the Captain evidently didn't expect any, or he wouldn't have taken to the wide ocean in a cockleshell lifeboat.

'I lay down on the rock and stared out over the flat, empty sea. I felt more miserable, lost and scared than I have ever been in all my life.

'"Alone!" I muttered – "Alone on an uninhabited island!"'

The Sea Dog paused a second or two with an odd stare in his eyes as if he saw again that vision of his own loneliness, on the uninhabited island. The audience, eager as it was for him to go on, waited with its usual patient respect till he should come out of his reverie. At length he shook himself a little, as though to throw off the gloom of his thoughts, and jerking up his head he continued.

'How long I sat on there I don't know. But finally I decided I had got to make the best of a bad job. To begin with, I thought I would explore the island thoroughly from end to end. There was much of it I had not yet seen. This bit of land was likely to be my home for some time to come. I had better know all there was to be known about it. I set out and in one day I travelled all around it. I found many interesting places: caves, bays, streams, cliffs and what not. I even came upon signs of human habitation, a long time disused; but whether they were relics of shipwrecked sailors or of native inhabitants of an earlier age, I could not

HUGH LOFTING

tell. At various points I established homes for myself – just shelters, you know, where I could take refuge any time when night overtook me in that part of the island. I marked these places and took careful note of their whereabouts so I'd remember how to get to them in case of need.

'I found there was lots of game on the island. Rabbits were plentiful. I noticed a kind of grouse, partridges, plovers, some geese and a great variety of sea birds. Many of these, as you know, build their nests on the ground among the stones of beaches or on rock ledges. And I made a note that their eggs would form a good article of diet at certain seasons of the year. There was also plenty of deer and larger game, but that I didn't bother with. I found the tracks of a few dangerous animals as well, what might be a puma or mountain cat of some sort. But I decided that with all the rabbits and birds to eat, these would not bother me.

'Next I began to plan out my day's work. With no company at all, I had to have something regular to do of course. I decided that since I couldn't signal to any passing boat, like a man could, the next best thing was to make sure that I didn't miss any that might come for water or fresh fruit. Such a thing was possible. The island was big enough. So in order to make sure that no vessels called without my knowing it, I established lookout stations on the summits of the hills that commanded a view of the sea all round the horizon. Also I planned to take note of the direction of the prevailing winds in order that scent might help me in detecting the approach of ships. I was going to make it a part of the daily programme to visit these lookout stations regularly.

'The next day it rained – miserably, steadily. This brought up another problem in my new wild life. I realized now fully for the first time what we dogs had done to ourselves by becoming part of human life instead of wild life – to which we at one time belonged. What about the weather? I had got to expect all sorts. It was autumn now. I had no idea what the winter in these parts might be like – certainly the nights were nippy enough already. And then food? That was another thing that must be thought of in connexion with the changing season. There was plenty now. But would the supplies be procurable later in the year? Maybe the birds left for other lands. Well, I calculated, there should always be rabbits. And though I was by this time heartily sick of the taste of rabbit – to this day the smell of 'em will make me run the other way for miles – I felt I should be easily able to manage till the season changed.

'But what I did do in preparation for colder weather was to line all my caves with thick beds of dry leaves and wild hay. Also I laid up a goodly store of wild corn in the husk. This I had found was good, nutritious chewing and grew in abundance in the swamp-flats on the southern side of the island.

'A week passed. I told myself that I could manage this kind of life as well as any wild dog – there are still some in Australia, you know. But was I lonely? – Oh dear! Don't speak of it. At the end of the week there came another rainy day. I slopped through the long round of my lookout posts. The sea was dark with rain and you couldn't see more than a mile or so, but I went the rounds anyway. Finally real darkness came on and I was glad to see it. I was wet, weary and wretched. Miserably I was toiling my way up the hills towards one of my higher caves. In the damp evening air all scents were very keen, and this made me remember that there were other beasts who had noses as keen as mine. For the present I wasn't going to trust these meat-eating animals till I knew their habits better. I was making for a certain deep hole in a rock wall where I knew no night-prowling enemy could take me by surprise.

'Suddenly on my way up the hillside I smelled *smoke*! From where could it come? No underbrush fire could start naturally on a day as wet as this had been. Maybe the island was inhabited after all. Native savages perhaps. If there were any they would of course stay hidden till the white men had left. Anyhow I must find out. Forewarned is forearmed. Through the dank twilight and the dripping wet underbrush I took up the trail of smoke, determined to see without being seen. It led me over the ridge in the middle of the island and down the other slope. On this coast broad sands spread themselves out at low tide a good mile in depth. From a shoulder I saw, away down below, the glimmer of a fire on the beach. One solitary figure, with his back to me, was squatting before the blaze motionless. Like a stalking wolf, yard by yard. I crept downwards, nearer. Finally in the still, wet darkness sounds came to me. The man was weeping. No, it wasn't a man: it was a boy. And what was this new scent coming with the smoke? ... Yes ... Yes, it was – *It was Snooky*. He must have missed the boats. He had delayed too long in facing the anger of the Captain and they had gone without him.

'I let out one tremendous bark of joy – like a pistol shot in the damp, silent night – and raced for the beach. I was alone no more!'

5

THE REMAINS OF THE 'SEA SWALLOW'

'WORDS cannot describe,' the Sea Dog continued, 'poor Snooky's joy at the sight of me. At first my bark nearly scared him to death, bursting as it did on the solemn silence of the sea and the rain-soaked island. But when he peered through the twilight and realized that it was I racing towards him across the sands of the beach, he flung his arms wide open with welcome.

'"Rover!" he cried. "Rover! I thought you had gone with the crew."

'Then he clutched me to his heart and wept and laughed over me, pouring forth the story of his search for me, of how he had missed the boats and decided when I did not answer his call that I had gone with them. Of course I could not make him understand why I had not answered, but he could tell anyway that I was tremendously glad to see him again.

'He looked starved. I knew that he had not the skill to

catch rabbits himself. A few shells scattered round the fire showed me that a small ration of oysters and such fish was probably all that he had had to eat in several days. I had a fine pair of fat rabbits stored away in a cave. These I went and got for him and we roasted them at the fire and ate them. Then I conducted him up the slope a little way to where I had one of my sleeping places, well lined with dry leaves and hay. There we made another fire with the matches which he had been careful to keep dry. Soon he spread his wet clothes before a cheerful blaze and from the shelter of the cave we watched them as they steamed. He had evidently lost heart at finding himself entirely deserted. But my reappearance seemed to put new life into him, and right away he became cheerfully busy doing all the little things that help to make life pleasant under conditions of hardship.

'As it was a little early to go to bed yet, I presently left him and went down to the beach to see what had been left by the crew.

'I had suspected that it wouldn't be much. And it was indeed precious little : a few old packing-cases, empty tins, bottles, and such rubbish. The tarpaulin was gone and all the foodstuffs. Away out in the gloom of the sea the masts of our stranded vessel were still visible. I hoped, as I turned back to go to bed, that the fair weather would hold long enough for Snooky and me to get to her before she was broken up by the waves.

'On my way back towards the cave I suddenly realized with a sort of guilty feeling that after all I had been responsible for Snooky's getting left behind. Firstly, if it hadn't been for me he would of course have stayed with the crew from the beginning. And secondly, if he hadn't wasted the whole day hunting over the island for me he would have rejoined them in time to catch the boats. But then, I reminded myself, if it hadn't been for my assistance he would most certainly have been drowned the night the ship was wrecked. And, as a matter of fact, as things turned out, my delaying his departure saved him a great deal of hardship and was the best thing that could have happened in the end.

'The next morning I was up bright and early and was greatly pleased to find that the weather was still fair. After our breakfast of cold roast rabbit I took Snooky down to the beach. The water was calm and smooth. I plunged in and started swimming out to the ship. A little puzzled, Snooky waited for me on the shore.

'I reached the *Sea Swallow* and scrambled on board. In the waist of the vessel I saw that there were still life-boats left in good condition, but so hopelessly tangled up with the gear that it would take a deal of work to launch them.

'Then I began barking to Snooky on the shore. He saw at once what I wanted, and taking off some of his clothes, he set out to swim to me. I went half way to join him and give him courage, and he made the trip all right, even if a bit winded.

'When he had got his breath back somewhat I showed him the lifeboats. And he promptly went to work to cut them loose from the tangle of ropes. He knew a good bit about seamanship, Snooky did, even if he was only an apprentice. Of course the boats were far too heavy for a man to lift them over the side single-handed. But by means of a block and tackle which he lashed to the mast-head he finally hoisted one boat's bow high in the air, and making it fast like that, he swung its stern over the side and lowered it into the water.

'All the oars had been taken away by the crew or washed overboard. But with the water calm, it was no great matter to paddle it as far as the land with such flat pieces of wood as we could tear loose from the broken ship. As soon as we

42

HUGH LOFTING

had her beached we dragged her well up out of reach of the surf and set about making better oars from the pieces of packing-cases which the crew had left upon the shore.

'And now, with a boat of his own, Snooky cheered up no end. Life was indeed made much easier and we felt that if the worst came to the worst we had something to put to sea in – though such a plan would of course be highly dangerous. The trip to and from the ship became a simple matter. We ransacked the old wreck from stem to stern and brought ashore hammers and axes and other tools with which to make things. We also found some foodstuffs the crew had overlooked which had not yet been ruined by the

HUGH LOFTING

sea : a sack of dried beans, a bag of flour – the inside part of which was still good – and a tin of ship's biscuit.

'In addition, we got several pieces of sailcloth, part of which we used to make a sail for our boat and part for a signal flag to attract passing ships.

'On one of the summits of the island there was an old dead pine tree. This Snooky stripped of its branches with a hatchet. And to its top he fastened an enormous flag. It was a distress signal which on a clear day could be seen for miles and miles.

'Then with pieces of plank we built ourselves a beach hut and furnished it with table and chair, and even with a few plates and dishes which we saved from the wreck. Altogether, after two days' work – which kept us occupied and cheerful – we felt we had a pretty decent home on our island and were prepared for almost anything. And when at last bad weather came along and a storm pounded the poor *Sea Swallow* to a litter of driftwood, we congratulated ourselves that we had got everything out of her that was of any use to us before it was too late.

'A week after that I noticed that Snooky was beginning to get miserable and downcast again. I tried to cheer him up by being as lively as possible myself. But I saw he was thinking of home and pining for human company. And it was evidently in his mind to put to sea in the boat – a foolhardy undertaking, which I had hoped he would put off till all hope of rescue had been abandoned. It seemed to me that for the present we were very well off where we were. With our new equipment, I felt we could carry on for months, if necessary, during which time some vessel would be sure to call and take us off.

'But almost every day Snooky would mess about with the boat, touching her up with tar, making masts for her and other things to fit her up for a voyage. I was against it. I was certain that to put to sea in such a little bit of a craft, with a crew of one, could only lead to disaster.'

6

SHIP AHOY!

'THE more Snooky thought about putting to sea the surer I became that it was the wrong plan for us to follow. I used to lie awake at night trying to think out things I could do to keep him from embarking on a voyage which I felt would mean certain destruction for both of us. I took several of the more important parts of the boat's furnishings – ropes, rowlocks, and the like – and hid them. He was kept busy renewing or providing makeshifts for these. And in that way I managed to delay him for several days.

'But I could not do this sort of thing too often without arousing his suspicions. And the day came when especially fine weather tempted him to make a start. So it seemed that the only course left was for me to disappear again. This I did. And poor Snooky, just as he was about to put to sea, had to go hunting and whistling all over the island for his dog.

'Neither could that device be repeated too often lest he decide one day that I had met with some accident and that it was useless for him to wait. Under cover of the bushes and woods I kept watch on him, and when I thought that he was about to give me up for lost I'd reappear again, trying to look as though I had just returned from a rabbit-hunting expedition.

'I did this twice and on the second occasion I thought I had lost him for good. I had gone off just at the moment when he seemed on the point of departure, and I calculated that I could give him at least two days to hunt for me before he'd decide to go alone. Well, while I was wandering around the far end of the island I saw a vessel off to the north-east and headed for our shores. I watched her for a minute till I was certain that she meant to visit us. Then, fairly bursting with the good news, I sped away to tell Snooky.

'When I got to the beach imagine my horror to find that he had gone! I sped at once up to one of my lookout stations, and from there I saw his boat, a mere chip in the wide ocean, far out to sea, making away with sail set. I barked and yelped for all I was worth. But even while I did it I knew that it was impossible for my voice to reach him at that range.

'Then I hustled back to meet the incoming ship. I knew Snooky could not have seen it yet, because the island lay between the vessel and him. My hope was that I could somehow make the crew understand that he had put to sea without seeing them and that he must be picked up at all cost.

'I was, of course, tremendously excited and anxious. First of all I was worried that the ship, seeing no sign of human life, might leave again right away, without perhaps even putting a boat ashore. Our flag after all might have been set up and left there by castaways years ago. And my other great fear was that Snooky might just go sailing on over the horizon and miss this one great chance of rescue.

'I watched the ship as she cautiously approached the island. Presently I could make out the man swinging the lead for soundings. And a little later, to my great delight, I saw them drop anchor and lower a boat.

'"Well," I thought to myself, "now they're here, they can't go away again in such a hurry. I'll have time to take another look at Snooky." And back I hurried once more to the lookout and scanned the sea to the sou'westward.

'To my horror, not a sign of the boat was anywhere visible! I could hardly believe he had had time to sail beyond the horizon. But there it was: he was gone. Maybe some accident had happened to him. Or perhaps a sudden stiff breeze had sprung up out there and carried him swiftly out of sight.

'Dismally at last I turned away from looking at the empty sea and made my way down towards that part of the shore where the ship's boat would most likely land. All my joy at the sight of her and the prospect of rescue was gone now. Yet, of course, it would have been madness to remain behind just because he was not to accompany me. I

would make friends with the boat's crew, I told myself, and they would, no doubt, take me off on to their ship.

'This I did. They were a nice lot of men. They took me into the little boat and then proceeded to row around the island to see if there was anyone else to be picked up. When they came in sight of our beach hut they went ashore again, taking me along in the hope that I'd guide them. But I just sat down on the sands to show them that any hope of human rescue was past.

'"He's the last of them," the men muttered, shaking their heads as they watched me. "Must be he's the only survivor, a dog!"

'Presently as we were getting back into the boat to go to the ship I suddenly startled them all by barking at the top of my voice. Round a little headland to the westward a small sailboat was tacking into the wind. It was Snooky! He hadn't gone at all. I imagine he had just wanted to scare me so I wouldn't delay him again. And coming back, keeping close inshore within the shelter of the land, his boat had been invisible from my lookout.

'That,' said the Sea Dog, 'is practically all of my story. When we reached the ship we were given a wonderful welcome and treated like heroes. Snooky soon forgave me for the various tricks I had played on him to delay his sailing. For had I not been the means of his getting a comfortable passage home after all? And as a matter of fact, he learned later that though the rest of the *Sea Swallow*'s crew had reached port, they only did so after weeks of terrible suffering and hardship. And from that, by combination of luck and management, he had been spared.

'For a good many voyages more we stuck together as shipmates. But at last I grew weary of the sea and gave up the life altogether.'

As the Sea Dog left the little platform at the end of the room, the noise of the applause was truly deafening. The deep barks of the big dogs mingled with the shrill yelps of the little ones, and the general chorus could be heard a mile away. The speaker had to come back on to the platform seven times to receive the appreciation of the audience before the noise finally subsided.

Then suddenly a new cry was taken up and repeated all about the hall:

'The Doctor! Speech, speech! The Doctor! Speech!'

John Dolittle had, in his interest in the story, long since forgotten the mission which had brought him tonight to the Home for Crossbred Dogs. Now that his presence in the hall had been thus publicly announced, the eyes of all were

turned on him and it became quite evident that he stood no chance whatever of escaping without first addressing the enthusiastic gathering. Bowing cheerily right and left, he made his way through a forest of wagging tails and flapping ears and stepped up on to the platform.

'Members,' said he, 'you must excuse me from any speech-making this evening. And after listening to the Sea Dog's yarn I do not feel that you are in any need of outside entertainment. At the Rat and Mouse Club we had a series of life stories told by the members. These were taken down by Manager Stubbins and later printed in Rat and Mouse language to become part of the club library. I think it would be a good idea if you did the same here. Your house committee can assist President Jip in making a selection. When the stories are told here I should very much like to be invited to attend. For the present, after thanking you for a pleasant evening, I must wish you good night.'

DAPPLE

I

THE CHAMPION

I THINK that of all my experiences as manager of the Dolittle Zoo I enjoyed those connected with the Home for Crossbred Dogs the most. Of course I had always known that there was a great variety in the characters and personalities of dogs; but I certainly never realized *how* great a variety till I began to take part in the daily life of this mongrels' club.

There was one member of the Home who was thoroughbred. This was Dapple the Dalmatian. Not only was he thoroughbred, he was a prizewinner with a pedigree ever so long and gold medals and ribbons and honourable mentions to his credit from nearly all the big dog shows. For these reasons he was not, strictly speaking, eligible as a member of the Home. And when he first arrived there were certain members who objected because he wasn't a mongrel. But Dapple explained to the committee that it wasn't after all his fault that he was born thoroughbred, and as he was already very popular with almost every dog in the club, he was finally accepted in spite of his aristocratic breeding.

He was one of those dogs whose coming to the Dolittle Zoo had caused the Doctor a good deal of trouble with their owners. Dapple belonged to a most extraordinary lady. She was very stout and used to make herself look still larger by the ruffles and frills she wore. Jip always said that she reminded him of an enormous, highly-scented cream puff. When Dapple first ran away to join the club she came after him (in a carriage and pair with two footmen) and took him

HUGH LOFTING

away again. She blamed the Doctor for his coming. But Dapple ran away so many times that finally she saw it was no use. It was clear that the dog himself preferred the simple joys of the mongrels' club to the extravagant luxury of her elaborate household. So, saying that the dog couldn't after all really be thoroughbred to desert *her* home for a mere zoo, she turned up her nose and bade her pet good-bye for the last time – to Dapple's great delight – and departed.

I don't just know how it came about, but this dog was elected to tell the second of the after-dinner stories (or autobiographies, as I called them in my book). And when John Dolittle and I came into the dining room the following evening, we found Dapple already installed on the speaker's platform and the rest of the club sitting around waiting. The committee did not want the story to begin till the Doctor and I should arrive.

Our appearance was welcomed with yelps of greeting and sighs of relief. I found myself a comfortable corner where I could spread out my papers for taking down the record. The Doctor was at once surrounded and carried off to another corner by all his adoring friends, who wanted to sit beside him. Silence gradually settled down over the dining room and Dapple began.

'I fancy,' Dapple said, 'that my story's chief interest for you will lie in the fact that it is the story of a thoroughbred's life. How often have I envied you happy mongrels! For my existence from the beginning was a monotonously thoroughbred existence. With my entrance into your club this week, I have, almost for the first time, obtained that liberty which you have enjoyed all your days.

'I will begin from the time when I and two of my brothers and two sisters found ourselves in a dog shop on sale. We were put into a little pen with straw on the bottom and 'PEDIGREED PUPPIES' written across the front. To begin with we didn't like it at all. But you know the way puppies are: it didn't take us long to forget our troubles and we soon began to play and wrestle together and had a pretty good time. The boy who looked after us and gave us our meals was a very nice lad; and whenever he wasn't busy he would join in our games.

'Customers would come into the shop and look at us. And one by one my brothers and sisters were all sold and I was the last to be left. I felt very sad about this at first. But the shop-boy did his best to console me and took me out for walks after his work was done.

' "Dapple," he used to say, "you're the best looking pup of the whole family. Those customers don't know anything about dogs – for all their knowing airs they put on – or they would never have left you to the last. But I'm glad they have. I wish I had the money to buy you myself. But you're so expensive. That's on account of your pedigree, you see. Five pounds. Think of it! For a little round dumpling like you! You should feel proud. And me only earning five shillings a week!"

'I used to watch the customers that came in. I grew to like the shop-boy more and more. And as time went on I became less and less anxious to be sold. I used to pretend to be very ill-natured so the customers wouldn't buy me. When they'd put their hands into the pen to stroke me I'd growl and show my teeth.

'"Oh!" they'd say. "Snappish, eh? No, I don't want that dog. Couldn't trust him with the children."

'And to my great relief they'd leave my cage and go on to look at the collie pups who lived next door to me. But one day a man came in whose cheerful smiling face I rather liked from the very beginning. As usual I growled to show that I wasn't to be trusted with children, as soon as he tried to pet me. But, to my great surprise, he took not the slightest notice. Maybe he didn't have any children. Anyway he seemed to know that I was just putting it all on, because instead of starting back and going away, he just laughed and went right on stroking me. And soon I gave up trying to scare him off and started to play. He seemed such a jolly, honest, nice man that I didn't mind even if he did buy me.

'Well, in the end the man bought me and took me away to his country home. It was a very nice home and I felt sure right from the start that I had been very lucky and was going to enjoy my life there. My owner seemed to be a sort of country gentleman – not terribly rich, but quite well off. He didn't work. His time was occupied fishing and hunting and looking after his very large and lovely country estate.

'It appeared that the shop-boy had been right and that I was destined to turn out a very specially fine specimen of the Dalmatian breed. As soon as I began to grow up a little all of my owner's friends who came to stay with him made flattering remarks about me and prophesied that I was surely going to be a prizewinner. In time my owner began entering me for dog shows. Oh, dear, how I hated those shows! For weeks beforehand I used to get dieted and scrubbed and brushed and trimmed and fixed so I would look my very best. I wasn't allowed to go out in muddy weather lest I mess up my immaculate coat or get my nails dirty. And when the show came off I had to sit for hours on a bench waiting for the silly judges to come around and examine me – when all I wanted was to be out in the nice wet fields chasing hares or digging for rats.

'I took many prizes – ever so many. I suppose, as such things go, I really had a wonderful career. For three years I carried off the highest honours in the Dalmatian class from every show I was entered for. My picture was in all the sporting papers. And I even had my portrait painted in oil colours by a famous artist. I got a stiff neck standing still while it was being done.

'But I didn't care for my show career a bit. My owner seemed to realize this and as soon as the shows were over he would always let me out in the fields to get as dirty as I liked and have a good time till the next show came along. It amused him. He even used to get dirty himself, helping me to dig for rats.

'This very nice man was fond of betting on the race horses. That was his ruin. He was just as unsuccessful on the race-track as he was successful at the dog shows. He lost and lost and lost. Soon he began to have to sell things to make good his losses. Part of his fine country estate was put on the market. Then some of his horses, beauties, they were. One thing after another went, but still he wouldn't stop

HUGH LOFTING

betting. He was always hoping that he'd make a big win and get back what he had lost.

'I began to wonder when I would get sold. I knew that at the shows he had been offered tremendous sums for me by millionaire dog fanciers. And much as he liked me – we were tremendous friends – it would only be natural, with all this need for money pressing on him, that some day he'd be tempted to part with me.

'After a few more months things got so bad that my owner was actually in want. There were many days when he didn't get enough to eat. And I created quite a sensation by bringing him home chickens which I took from the poulterer's shop in the village as I passed. It never occurred to me, I'm afraid, that there was anything wrong in my taking them. But the poulterer seemed to think there was. And I realized, after I had been caught and taken to the police station a second time, that I was giving my owner a good deal more trouble than profit.

'Of course as things went from bad to worse it began to look quite unavoidable that I must be sold. For even some of his household servants had not been paid their wages in a very long time.

'The day came. A woman who had often admired me at the shows offered a particularly high price when the poor man was at his wits' end for money. He made the farewell short — for which I was glad. Neither of us cared for emotion or a show of sentiment, and if I had to go I wanted to do so quickly and as quietly as possible.

' "I'm sorry, Dap," said he, giving me a final pat on the head. "I feel horribly guilty, selling you. But — well, good-bye and good luck to you, old boy."

'I felt dreadfully sad — and resentful, too. Not against him, for I saw that as the situation was it couldn't be helped now, but against my pedigree. If I hadn't been so beastly well bred my value would have been only a few shillings. And it would have hardly been worth anyone's while to sell me.

'As I was led away by my new fat mistress I muttered to myself, "Oh, why, *why* wasn't I born a mongrel?"

'Then my life entered upon an entirely new chapter. The woman who bought me was fabulously rich. She had enough servants and carriages and silver dishes and porcelain bath-tubs for six people. I shall never forget my disgust the first evening when I was brought to her home. Tea was being served and her drawing room was full of women guests, all jabbering and munching cakes. She had me led in to show me off to them.

' "My dears," she cackled, "isn't he a beauty? I paid a terrible price for him. But I just *had* to have him — to go with my new gown, you know. The spots on his coat match the polka-dot silk perfectly — just perfectly!" '

2

A WILD BREAKFAST PARTY

'CAN you imagine my disgust?'

Dapple's elegant, well-bred nose seemed to curl upward with scorn as he appealed to his audience. He was surely a beautiful creature to look at. Dalmatians were a more popular breed then than they are now. As a boy I had always called them 'plum-pudding dogs', on account of their black spots. But I don't know that I had ever seen a thoroughbred champion before. And certainly such a homely title did not seem at all fitting for as fine a dog as this.

'That was what I had come to,' he went on. 'That was all my wellbredness and pedigree were to mean in the end: to be bought by an hysterical, cackling, empty-headed woman *because I matched her new polka-dot gown!* The shame of it — for a sporting dog like me! I was now to be part of a boudoir's furnishings. I ground my teeth with rage. And that very night of my arrival was the first time I ran away — the first time out of a dozen.

' "So I'm to match a polka-dot dress, am I?" I muttered furiously. "All right. Then I'll get rid of my spots."

'I knew John Dolittle well, of course, and I came straight to his home as soon as I got away.

' "Doctor," I said, "I want you to paint out my spots, or dye me a new colour, or something. I just will not be part of that woman's wardrobe. She wants to take me out on a

string so people will stare at us and say how smart she is. You must do something. I simply can't bear the thought – the fat nincompoop!"

'Well, the Doctor sympathized with me and I do believe he might have done it if he hadn't had so many rows already about dogs running off from their owners to come and join his club in the Zoo here. I hung around still trying to persuade him, and while I was at it the wretched woman herself turned up to claim me. She had had me traced by droves of detectives. She is so horribly rich.

'So back I had to go to my doom as a boudoir ornament. She hugged me and kissed me with joy at getting me back.

Then she put some perfume on me. She said I ought to use the same perfume as she wore. Think of it : me – *perfumed*!

'Oh, I forgot to mention that this woman had a husband. It isn't any wonder that I forgot to mention him, because he really wasn't of any account anyway. He was just a husband to her – and a nuisance to me. He used to get bossed and hen-pecked to death by his wife and I suppose he felt *he* had to boss some one, so he tried to boss me. She used to send him to take me out for runs in the evening and he was always trying to teach me silly tricks which I didn't want to know, shouting orders at me in a loud voice so the passers-by could see what a masterful character he was. He would send me on errands to fetch his walking-stick, which he would deliberately leave behind against a tree or a wall. So silly! I usually brought back a dead rat, if I could find one, or a banana skin instead. I already knew a whole lot of good tricks. But the only fun I got out of these was trying to spoil his show and appearing as stupid as I could possibly be. Then he used to make me carry his newspaper in my mouth, but I always dropped it in the first puddle I passed.

'What a life! And how I longed to get away from it! One of the most terrible things about it was that I began to find my own character changing. My old owner had been a healthy, outdoor man of a calm, sensible disposition. With him I had grown into a sensible, sporting country dog. Now, being constantly with this hysterical woman who was always weeping over me – she insisted on telling me all her troubles, which were wholly imaginary and quite tiresome – I found to my horror that I was becoming a snappy, irritable, spoiled lap-dog. Like her, in fact. It was a dreadful discovery. I was always running away, but I always got brought back again. My one ambition was to get into the Doctor's club here and become once more a calm, sensible, worth-while dog. Then I thought that maybe I'd have better luck if I went back to my old owner next time I escaped. I

61

foam with lather. It wasn't pleasant but it looked wonderful.

'"Good!" I said to myself as I went to bed that night after my secret rehearsal. "Tomorrow I'll be a mad dog. Then they'll *have* to get rid of me."

'I have done a few crazy things in my life,' the Dalmatian continued, 'but never, I think, anything quite so crazy as pretending I was a real crazy dog. It is a wonder I'm alive. You see, with the case I had seen on the streets – when the mad dog went running round with staring eyes and frothing mouth – things happened differently. The people just fled away from him, scared blue. I didn't know that it is the custom to shoot mad dogs. I suppose nobody had a gun handy that time. But this time they had – several.

'Well, to begin from the beginning: I had timed my outbreak of madness to take place while my mistress was having breakfast. I had kept my piece of shaving soap handy from the night before, and while she was drinking her first cup of coffee I got it all frothy in my mouth. It was her habit to give me a lamb cutlet at breakfast time. She had no idea of feeding dogs. I was already losing my figure from being continually fed between meals. That's how she lost her figure too – if she ever had one – by eating tit-bits at odd times. So my lamb cutlet, specially cooked, was brought in by the footman on a silver tray in the usual manner, and my mistress took it by the paper frill and called to me:

'"Come along, Dappy darling," said she. "Mama give little Dapsy his breakfast."

'That's the way she used to talk. It almost spoiled my appetite many a time. I came up to her, but instead of taking the cutlet, I took her hand in my teeth – not to bite her, really, you understand. Poor old thing, she certainly meant to be kind enough. But I had to play the part of a mad dog properly. She started back with a scream. Then I snarled and big gobs of white soapsuds slobbered from my mouth.

63

I rolled my eyes. Then I threw a somersault and bit the carpet. Next I bit the footman in the leg – I owed him one anyway. Then I bit the table in the leg and the breakfast dishes capsized with a crash on to the floor. After that I leapt on to the sofa and let out a bloodcurdling howl like a lost wolf.

'My mistress sprang up and ran for the door. The footman had already jumped through the window – into a bed of geraniums.

'"Oswald!" the woman shrieked – that was her husband's name – "Oswald! Come quick! The dog's gone mad!"

64

3

MAD DOG!

'WELL, Oswald came. But he didn't stay very long. I made one snarling rush at him and he, too, dived through the window into the geraniums.

'Then the butler arrived on the run. Bells were ringing, doors slamming and people yelling all over the house by this time. The butler was a fat and pompous booby. He was armed with a golf club. I tore his pants for him as soon as he appeared, and all he succeeded in doing with the golf club was to smash a couple of valuable vases on the mantelpiece. He, too, beat a hasty retreat – to get more help, he said. Meantime I rushed round the breakfast room in circles, tossing cushions in the air, tearing down the curtains, upsetting furniture, howling, blowing soap bubbles all over the place. Oh, I was the grandest thing in mad dogs you ever saw.

'The trouble was I was too good. After I had thoroughly wrecked the breakfast room I dashed out into the hall, pulling down a hatrack playfully as I passed, and from there I rushed on into the garden. In the garden, for the first time, I realized what I had done. All over the place, behind bushes and trees and things, I saw men lurking with guns. *Bang! Bang!* . . . *Bang! Bang!* I was fired on from all sides. The noise was like a war. How I escaped goodness only knows. She had about twenty gardeners, but I suppose that they were all, luckily, bad shots. They didn't hit me. The only one that got hit was the butler – in the pants, the same pants that I had already torn. He got over it all right. But, poor man, it was his unlucky day.

'I sped right down to the end of the garden, making for a

gate whose bars I knew I could get through. I reached it in safety, gained the road and raced away in the direction of the Doctor's house. Behind, the yells and shots of the enemy followed hot on my heels.

' "Mad dog!" they bawled. "Look out! His bite's poisonous! Shoot him! Mad dog!"

'Everyone ahead of me ran for their gates, climbed lampposts, popped behind doors, leapt over walls, anything to get away from poor me, the enemy of society. It began to look as though I had been a bit too clever and that my grand plan might cost me my life.

' "The Doctor," I kept muttering to myself as I stretched out at full speed. "He's my one chance. He can explain to these idiots. The Doctor! I'll be all right if I can only reach John Dolittle's house before they fill my hide full of lead."

'As I raced down the road I began to wonder not only whether I was really crazy myself, but also whether the whole world had gone crazy, too. I'm sure, at all events, that that's what anyone coming suddenly upon the scene would have thought. The cry of "Mad dog!" was taken up and passed from house to house, so that the news of my coming actually got ahead of me, and soon I found myself beset behind and before. People leaned out of second-storey windows and threw flower-pots at me off the sills as I passed; policemen shot at me with pistols; one fellow tried to lasso me with a rope; another drove a big van across the road to head me off. Every man's hand was against me.

'But somehow, through the whole gauntlet, I wriggled and darted and jumped and squirmed. In my excitement I swallowed my shaving soap, which made me feel deathly ill, but, of course, I couldn't stop.

'Luckily for me, the noise and hubbub had brought the Doctor to his gate before I got there. And as soon as he saw it was me that was being chased he opened the gate, let me slip in and closed it behind me. Bullets and buckshot spattered against the stone coping of the wall as I sped up the steps, across the garden and into the house. The Doctor – I wonder he wasn't killed himself – raised his hands in truce and walked half way down the steps to meet my pursuers.

'"That dog is mad!" yelled one of the gardeners, rushing up with a gun. "What did you let him into your house for? He might bite someone!"

'Of course in less than five minutes there was a crowd around the foot of the steps like a theatre crush. Everybody talked at once. Some demanded that I be brought out and shot at once. And just as it began to look as though the crowd might thrust John Dolittle aside and take the law into its own hands my mistress arrived with her husband and a whole army of men servants.

'Of course the Doctor had guessed right away that I was pretending – even before I gasped it out as I sped by him up the steps. He planted himself firmly in front of the closed gate and faced Oswald the husband, who had now, with a dozen flunkeys at his back, become very brave.

'"You have my dog, sir!" said he, shaking his fist in the Doctor's face. "The dog is mad. It bit my wife and several of the servants. It must be destroyed at once. Let us in, please."

'"Pardon me," said the Doctor very politely – I was listening in great anxiety just below the study window – "the dog may be yours, but these premises are mine. You cannot come in. Now just calm down a moment and let us talk this over."

'"I will not listen to you," cried the valiant Oswald. "The dog is a danger to public health. It must be destroyed. It bit my wife who, in spite of her injury, has come here to see that no one else is harmed. The dog must be destroyed at once – immediately." '

4

THE DOCTOR GIVES A LECTURE

'BY this time the crowd had grown still larger, all the stragglers having come up to be in at the kill. And things began to look really serious for the Doctor. A couple of old farmers in the rear began to harangue the mob, encouraging them to rush the gate. From my hiding place behind the study window I saw the crowd surge forward suddenly. I was still panting, breathless, from my long run. And the prospect of having to break out at the back of the house and be chased some more was not at all pleasant.

'But the Doctor wasn't to be easily brushed aside. He suddenly snatched a gun from the hands of one of the gardeners, and, bringing it to his shoulder, he faced the mob.

'"Stand back – everybody!" he commanded shortly. "This is my home and no one can enter it without a search-warrant signed by a magistrate."

'At that, greatly impressed, the mob fell back instantly. I wondered what was going to happen next. But before the Doctor could say any more my mistress suddenly fainted into her husband's arms. I suppose she had just remembered how seriously she'd been wounded. Anyway, she nearly squashed poor Oswald, who was a small, frail man, with her enormous weight.

'That took the general attention off the "mad dog" for the moment. The Doctor, calling to Dab-Dab to bring some water from the house, personally attended to the lady and she was soon brought round.

'Then he gave her a lecture. He assured her as a doctor and a veterinary surgeon that I wasn't mad at all. He told

her kindly but firmly that she didn't know anything whatever about bringing up dogs – that he was well acquainted with me and was sure that she had ruined my disposition by turning me from a sporting outdoor dog into a silly boudoir pet.

'"So you see, Madam," he concluded, "instead of being mad or having rabies, Dapple has merely started the habit of – er – hysterics – which, in fact, he has caught from you. Hysterics, Madam, you should know, while a very minor disorder, is highly contagious."

'Some of the policemen had now arrived. And the farmers had been urging them to go in and get me. But when it became known that the little man defending his home with such firmness was a Doctor of Medicine, a veterinary surgeon and a naturalist of great renown, the attitude of the whole crowd became entirely different. With such an authority maintaining that I was *not* mad, who would dare to invade his home and shoot me?

'"I am quite willing," said the Doctor, turning to the policemen, "to assume entire responsibility for the dog – provided this lady will leave him in my care. And I think, Madam," he added, addressing my mistress, "that you have had abundant proof that the dog does not like the home you have given him. This, as you know, is the fourth or fifth time that he has run away and come to me for refuge. Don't you think that it would be more humane and best from all points of view if you left him here?"

'"For my part," Oswald began, suddenly recovering from his squashing, "I wouldn't have the wretched cur in the house again for anything. I would sooner ..."

'His enormous wife turned and glowered on him and the poor little man shrivelled and subsided.

'"Oswald," said she, "this is my affair." She turned to the Doctor. "I am very disappointed in the dog," she said. "He was sold to me as a thoroughbred. He couldn't have been that to prefer such a place as this" – with a magnificent gesture she waved a fat arm towards the Doctor's small and modest house – "to my home. I never wish to set eyes on the ungrateful creature again. I couldn't have treated a child of my own with greater kindness."

'She began to weep.

'"But don't you see?' said the Doctor, advancing towards her full of sympathy. "That was just the trouble. You were too kind to him. He didn't want to be spoiled. He wished to be himself. He—"

'The woman waved him aside.

'"Enough!" she cried. "You may keep him. I never wish

70

to see the ungrateful creature again – Oswald, lead me to my carriage."

'And thereupon, behind the curtain of the study window, I threw a somersault for sheer joy as the portly lady got into her victoria and drove away – for good – leaving me in John Dolittle's home ... I am quite myself again now. But I believe I'd have become a real mad dog if I had stayed with her much longer ... truly the Doctor is a great man.'

THE DOG AMBULANCE

I

THE FIRST PATIENT

I T was about this time that the Dog Ambulance was started. This institution (the idea, you may remember, was originally Jip's) belonged to, and was organized entirely by, the Club. It was the first thing of its kind in history. And I felt that a description of it and the events that accompanied its inauguration could quite fittingly be included in my book, *Tales of the Home for Crossbred Dogs*. On consulting Jip I found that he agreed with me and we decided to put it in following the Dalmatian's story.

For several days in succession we had had serious cases of dog casualties on the streets: dogs run over; dogs kicked by horses; sick and homeless strays, etc. Many of these cases when brought to the surgery were so far gone that the Doctor had a hard time pulling them through.

'Tommy,' said Jip, coming to me at breakfast one morning, 'we've got to have a dog ambulance. I'm sure we can get the Doctor to agree to it because I've already spoken to him about it – the time we brought Kling here when he was poisoned – and he thought it was a good idea. In the Home, we have a couple of mongrel greyhounds. They're kind of funny to look at, but they're awful speedy. They have already volunteered to take it in turns doing duty. So we will have no difficulty with that part of it. What we need is the ambulance carriage itself and some harness for the greyhounds. Do you think you could build us a carriage and get your father to make us a set of harness?'

'Well, Jip,' I said, 'I don't know. But I am quite willing to try.'

So that same evening I went over to the Stubbins' cobbler shop where I found that my father, though he was pretty busy, would make us the harness in his spare time. Then I set to work with Bumpo, the African Prince, who prided himself on being something of a mechanic, and out of a pair of rubber-tyred perambulator wheels, a few springs out of an old bed and some pieces of packing-case, we constructed a very decent looking runabout, light enough to be drawn by a dog. We painted it white, put a red-cross flag on it and a bell. It was quite an elegant turnout.

When the harness was ready we hitched up one of the mongrel greyhounds, and Jip, as assistant casualty surgeon, drove around the zoo enclosure at a speed of thirty miles an hour – greatly to the astonishment of the inhabitants of Animal Town.

All concerned were very proud of the new Dog Ambulance. Night and day, from then on, one of the greyhounds was kept harnessed up in readiness to answer an emergency call.

'That's fine, Tommy,' said Jip – 'something that was really needed. Those serious cases can be brought to the surgery now with the least possible delay.'

Well, as such things often happen, now that we had a brand-new Dog Ambulance ready for all emergencies, we got no cases to try it out on. Suddenly all dog casualties seemed to cease. The gallant greyhound steeds stood in the harness from dawn to dark and never a call came for their services.

Jip, Kling and Toby, the chief organizers of the Animal Town First Aid, were dreadfully disappointed. Finally Jip became so anxious to try out the new ambulance that he and Toby decided secretly between them that if no case came along soon they would have to make one.

After many days of idle waiting they had (without telling either the Doctor or me) proudly led their ambulance out through the streets of Puddleby on their own. This they did partly because they wanted the townsfolk to see the elegant equipage in all its glory, and partly because they might find a 'case' by chance to try it on.

While they were parading through the town they came upon Gub-Gub, the Doctor's pet pig, in a back street sitting on a garbage heap. He was a great garbage-heap explorer, was Gub-Gub. The poor pig had eaten some bad turnips and was looking rather green in the face from a slight stomach-ache.

74

'Ah! A serious case!' cried Jip, rushing the ambulance up alongside the garbage heap in grand style. Then with great dispatch Orderlies Kling and Toby, under the direction of Surgeon Jip, pounced upon the wretched Gub-Gub and began hauling him on to the ambulance. They would have sooner had a dog patient to try their new equipment on, but a pig was better than nothing.

'Leave me alone!' bawled Gub-Gub, kicking out in all directions. 'I've only got a stomach-ache. I don't want to go in your ambulance!'

'Don't listen to him,' ordered Jip. 'He's delirious. Appendicitis most likely. It's a rush case, men. Get him on quick!'

The three of them rolled Gub-Gub's portly carcass on to the ambulance. Jip sprang into the driver's seat while Toby and Kling sat on the 'delirious' patient to hold him down.

Like a shot out of a gun the mongrel greyhound bounded away at full speed for the Doctor's home. Meanwhile Jip clanged the bell for all he was worth to clear the road ahead and drown the bellowings of the first case to be brought to the Dolittle surgery by the Dog Ambulance.

2

THE MISHAP AT KINGSBRIDGE

IT was a thrilling ride – thrilling for the staff of the ambulance, for the townsfolk who looked on and, most of all, for the patient. Certainly all records established up to that date were easily broken so far as sheer speed was concerned. But as to time – from picking up a case to delivery at hospital – that was another matter. Indeed, the original case never reached the surgery at all – in the ambulance. But I must tell the story in the proper order.

Streaking up the High Street with clanging bell, the

HUGH LOFTING

strange vehicle shot under horses' noses, past traffic policemen who ordered it to stop, round corners on two wheels,
scattering scared pedestrians right and left. At Kingsbridge
it met with its first accident. Here the road narrowed as it
crossed the river. In trying to avoid a pedlar's barrow the
greyhound steed went a shade too near a lamp-post. With
Gub-Gub's extra heavy weight added to that of the two
orderlies and the surgeon, the springs of the ambulance
were being taxed to their utmost anyway. The hub of the
right rear wheel only just touched the base of the lamp-
post. But it was enough to throw the overloaded, careening
carriage off its balance. On one wheel it shot across the

road and dumped its entire contents, surgeon, orderlies and patient, over the parapet of the bridge.

As it happened, the river was at low tide. At such time, wide stretches of black mud margined the narrow, swiftly running stream. This in a way was providential – for the patient, but not for the staff. Gub-Gub's rating as a swimmer was very low, and had the river been at high tide he would have had a hard time reaching the bank. Jip, Kling and Toby, on the other hand, would have much preferred a clean bath to the fate that awaited them below the bridge. All four landed with an oozy splash into the tidal mud. It broke the fall nicely, but it didn't improve their appearance. Entirely black from head to foot, the gallant staff still remembered its duty to the injured and proceeded to dig the struggling, squealing patient out of his mud bath.

Fortunately, the distance to firmer ground was not more than a few yards. Somehow the patient, who on account of his weight had sunk deeper in than the others, was hauled and dragged to solid territory. He may not have been a proper case for the ambulance when they had forcibly carried him off from the garbage heap, but by the time they had got him out of the mud of the river he was in considerably greater need of attention.

Regaining the bridge, the staff, now completely garbed in a new uniform of black mud, rolled the patient back on to the ambulance, jumped in after him and went away as fast as ever. In fact, they went even faster, for their mishap at the river had caused quite a crowd to collect and they were afraid they might be stopped at any minute.

For about a mile all went well. But as they turned into the Oxenthorpe Road at full gallop they met with still another accident. A sleek, overfed Pomeranian was crossing the road with great dignity. Suddenly, seeing the extraordinary carriage bearing down upon him at thirty-five miles an hour, he lost what little wits he had, ran first this way and then that and finally wound up under the front wheels of the ambulance. The carriage did not entirely capsize, but it tipped up sufficiently as it went over him to shoot the patient out again – this time into the gutter. The fiery greyhound steed was brought to a standstill and that keen – perhaps too keen – medical student, Jip, ran back to take charge of the situation.

The patient was lying on his back in the gutter, his four trotters waving in the air, yelling blue murder. Up the middle of the road the fat Pomeranian was also lying on his back and howling – mostly with indignation and fright. Surgeon Jip and Orderlies Toby and Kling held a hasty professional consultation. The ambulance could hardly take both casualties. Their first duty was to their original patient. On the other hand, the Dog Ambulance was originally intended for dogs, and here was a fine case ready at hand.

However, while the discussion was still going on, Gub-Gub, fearing he might have to continue his hazardous ride in the ambulance, suddenly sprang up and took to his heels. Sore as he was from his fall and his stomach-ache, he had had enough of Jip's first aid.

This solved the problem for the staff of the Dog Ambulance very nicely. Jip grabbed the Pomeranian by the scruff of the neck and, carrying him like a puppy, dumped him into the ambulance, sprang in once more and gave the word to go.

It wasn't until after the flying carriage had done another mile that he suddenly realized that he had left his two orderlies behind. But Kling and Toby, by putting on their best speed, came in on foot a very good second and third in the race for the surgery.

3

THE RECEPTION AT THE SURGERY

JIP, Kling and Toby were all sadly disappointed at the Doctor's reception of the Dog Ambulance the first time it returned from active service. I am bound to say that the equipage had lost much of its original smartness. The wheels were bent and wobbly, the bell post was twisted up like a corkscrew and the bell gone, the first-aid box beneath the driver's seat had burst open and bandages were trailing from it in the dust of the road behind. As for the staff, caked with mud and dust from head to foot, well, you could just tell that they were dogs and that was all.

The patient, as soon as the ambulance came to a halt, got out of the stretcher without waiting for assistance and at once began a long and indignant speech to the Doctor. He accused Jip and his assistants of first knocking him down by reckless driving and then kidnapping him right in front of his own gate.

No sooner had he finished his tirade than his mistress, who had followed in a cab, appeared upon the scene and began another long accusation. She assured the Doctor that she had heard a good deal about him and his crazy wild animals and she meant to appeal to the police. Things had come to a pretty pass, she said, when a man trained a gang of dogs to kidnap and steal other dogs.

The Doctor was just getting ready to answer her when Gub-Gub arrived, howling like a lost child who had been punished for something he never did. He began the third discourse upon the wicked deeds of the Red Cross Brigade who had carried him off against his will, thrown him over a bridge into the river, then rushed him over bumpy streets a few more miles and finally pitched him out into the gutter.

By the end of the last of these speeches the staff of the Dog Ambulance was beginning to feel that its services in the public good had been somewhat misdirected and not wholly understood. The greyhound steed slunk away to the zoo enclosure, where Bumpo undid his harness and separated him from the dilapidated carriage. As for Jip, Kling and Toby, they made no attempt to explain to the Doctor, but went miserably down to the fish pond and washed the mud from themselves. Not a word was said till they were on their way back to supper. Then Jip broke the silence with, 'We shouldn't have started with that ridiculous pig. He always puts a hoodoo on everything.'

THE STUNNED MAN

I

THE ROBBERY

KLING, who came to be known as the Detective Dog, lived at Doctor Dolittle's Home for Crossbred Dogs.

Gub-Gub, who dearly loved a mystery, tried to get Kling started on some new plot, because he was anxious to see a real detective at work. And by chance his wish was presently granted in a rather peculiar way.

Jip, who had been nosing about the neighbourhood in search of a bone he'd buried and lost, came upon a man lying in the middle of the road, unconscious. He immediately routed us out of bed and led us to the stranger.

Once more fate had pushed John Dolittle, willynilly, into the affairs of his neighbours. For, of course, even if he had not been a doctor, he would not have refused first aid to the injured at his door. Bumpo, who was living with us at the time, and I helped him carry the man in and lay him on the table in the surgery.

The man was not seriously injured, though from the tremendous bump on the back of his head I had at first thought he might be. The Doctor brought him round after a few moments. And the first thing he said when he opened his eyes was: 'I've been robbed. A lot of money has been stolen from me.'

'Ah!' said Gub-Gub, who was listening at the surgery door, 'the mystery of the stunned man. Good! I'll get Kling.'

The man seemed from his appearance to be a groom or stableman of some kind. As soon as he had gathered his

wits together a little he began pouring out the story of his troubles without waiting for any questioning or encouragement from the Doctor.

'I had forty pounds with me,' he said, 'what the boss had given me to take to the bank at Oxenthorpe. I had just stopped a minute to tie my bootlace outside your gate here when someone hit me a terrible blow on the head from behind. Then all was darkness till I woke up here. There will be an awful row when the boss finds out the money's gone. You'll stand by me, sir, won't you? You'll bear witness to what I say? Be you a doctor, sir?' he ended, looking round the surgery at the bandages and bottles.

'Er-yes, I'm a doctor,' said John Dolittle. 'But why be anxious? Your story will, no doubt, be believed – so long as you state it exactly as it happened. All we know is that we found you unconscious in the road. We can't bear witness to anything further than that. If you were robbed it is quite possible that the police may be able to get the money back for your employer.'

Gub-Gub, the pig, emerged from under the surgery table and nudged the Doctor's leg.

'I've brought Kling,' said he. 'He'll soon solve this.'

'No,' whispered the Doctor quickly. 'This is the police's affair, not ours. We will stay out of it.'

'Well, you see,' the man went on, 'you never can tell. The boss might even say that I stole the money. But you'll stand by me, won't you, Doctor?'

'I'll do what I said,' the doctor answered, apparently somewhat annoyed. 'I can't do any more. But don't be worried. Tell your employer the truth and I'm sure that everything will come out all right. Do you feel steady enough to walk now?'

The man got down from the table and tried a few paces.

'Yes,' he said, 'I reckon I can manage now. Thank you, Doctor. I'll be going. But maybe I'll have to call on you as a witness later.'

'That's all right,' said John Dolittle. 'I'm very busy, but I'll be willing to state what little I know of the case. Do you want me to send a message to have them come fetch you?'

'No, thank you,' said the man. 'I can walk.'

As we followed the man out into the garden and watched him descend the steps, I noticed that Kling and Jip were examining the road opposite the gate with great care. Gub-Gub, deeply interested in the proceedings, was looking on. But the two dogs made him keep his distance; they were evidently anxious that no meddling pig's trotters should spoil the tracks in the dust.

Directly the man had disappeared the Doctor hurried away to his study to get in a few minutes' work at his books before breakfast; while I, to kill time till Dab-Dab, the Duck-Housekeeper, should summon us to the kitchen, strolled down on to the road to watch the detective dog's investigations. Jip came up to me as I reached the foot of the steps and spoke in whispers, looking backward over his shoulder with respectful awe at Kling, the great expert.

'He's marvellous, Tommy,' he said – 'simply marvellous. He has already found out that half what that fellow told us wasn't true and that there were a whole lot of other things he didn't tell us at all. For one, he had a horse with him.'

'Goodness! Perhaps he was a highwayman,' put in Gub-Gub, who had sneaked up and joined us. Jip ignored the remark with contempt.

'I thought I was pretty good at tracks myself,' he went on. 'But compared with Kling, I'm just a beginner. On this case he hasn't said very much so far. But it's my opinion that he already has the whole thing straightened out in his mind.'

As a matter of fact Kling, since he had left the police service in Belgium, had not, he admitted, had any desire to return to that kind of work. It was now quite clear to me that the flattering admiration of Gub-Gub and Jip had been too much for the famous dog detective and had got him started on his old profession again. After breakfast the two dogs disappeared (no doubt on business connected with 'the case'); and it did not seem to me that any harm could be done so long as they didn't drag the Doctor into it.

But the next morning Dab-Dab woke me up in a great state of indignation.

'Tommy,' said she, 'you must make those wretched dogs stop this detective rubbish. What do you think they've done now?'

'I've no idea, Dab-Dab,' I said, sitting up and rubbing my eyes sleepily – 'No idea at all.'

'Well, come down to the porch and look,' said she.

Still only partly awake, I threw on some clothes and followed her downstairs.

'Open the front door,' said she.

I did so. And an enormous pile of old, disreputable-looking shoes, which had evidently been stacked up against the door, spilled into the hall. While up the path from the gate Jip and Kling were just arriving, each with another old shoe in his mouth, to add to the pile they had collected.

'Good gracious, Kling!' I cried. 'What's this? Anyone would think that the Doctor had gone into the second-hand clothes business from the mess you've made of the porch.'

'Sh! Tommy,' whispered Jip. 'Close the door and come outside a minute. Kling will explain.'

'Explain! Rubbish!' squawked Dab-Dab angrily. 'Kling just brought those shoes here to chew. He's as bad as Gub-Gub and his vegetable mysteries. If you dogs don't clear that mess off my porch before breakfast you won't get any – no, nor any lunch neither,' she added as I closed the door on her wrath and followed the dogs down the path.

2

THE FOOTPRINT IN THE COPSE

WITHOUT further word the two of them led me out on to the road, turned to the right and took me about a quarter of a mile in the direction of Oxenthorpe. Then, through a farm gate, they jumped into a meadow and struck out across it towards a copse in the middle. Looking around to make sure that no one should see us enter, they finally

led me into this through a hole in the surrounding hedge. Inside there was a clear open space beneath the trees where the earth was damp, mossy and practically grassless.

'This,' said Kling, leading me across to the foot of an oak tree, 'is where the money was buried. In fact, there is the money itself – in that bag.'

The earth here was all dug up where the dogs had evidently rooted down following a scent. Among the loose earth there was a small linen bag. I picked it up and shook it. It jingled with the sound of gold.

'Now, Tommy,' said Kling, 'come over here.'

I followed him a few yards away from the tree to where

a mossy hollow spread its green freshness beneath tall over-hanging hawthorns. It was a place which in wetter weather would have been a pond or bog.

'You see that?' asked Kling, pointing with his nose.

'Yes,' said I, 'a footprint.'

'Well, that's what we collected the shoes for,' said he. 'We want a shoe to fit that print.'

'But how on earth,' I asked, 'do you expect to find it – out of all the shoes in the world?'

'We don't,' said Kling with the patient air of a professor arguing with an obstinate, stupid child. 'We don't expect to find it among all the shoes in the world, but only among the shoes that were thrown away last night in this immediate neighbourhood. Which is a very different matter. We know that the man who made this print threw his shoes away, because when we followed up the tracks and scent we found that he had done part of his journey in stockinged feet. That's why we've gone round collecting all the shoes we could find under hedges and everywhere. And now we want you to pick out from the pile we've gathered a shoe that fits that print.'

'But why, Kling,' I asked, 'would not the scent you followed have led you to the man, even more surely than your knowing who it was that made this footprint?'

'Scents are freakish things,' said Kling, frowning. 'It was clear and distinct this far and led us, as easy as pie, to where the money was buried – and even beyond it for a way. But we lost it about a half-mile from here. We lost the stocking-feet tracks, too. The man, whoever he was, knew something about covering his own trail – probably an old criminal.'

'Then you don't think that the fellow that Jip found in the road could have hidden the money himself?' I asked.

'Certainly not,' said Kling quickly. 'We made a note of his scent when he was in the surgery. Whether he was in partnership with the man who took the money away and buried it, I have yet to find out. I suspect he was. Because the story he told the Doctor was *not* a frank statement at all. But he was not the one who brought the money here and buried it. That was done by the party who made that footprint. And then, I imagine, realizing that he had left tracks behind him, he got scared, took his shoes off and threw them away.'

'But how do you know that he threw them away?' said I. 'Why couldn't he have carried them in his hand?'

'Of that,' said Kling, 'we are not as yet absolutely sure. But we are pretty certain. For one thing, if he was afraid of the tracks giving him away to the police – he had made a whole lot of footprints in a field close to where the man was struck down – he would be afraid to have the shoes in his home. For another, he was already burdened with a spade, and perhaps other tools to do his digging with. It is certain that he was not far from home or he would never have attempted to make the return journey in his stockinged feet.'

'Do you think,' I asked, 'that he himself might have struck the man Jip found while quarrelling over the gold or something?'

'Perhaps, but I don't think so,' said Kling. 'It is more likely, in my opinion, that he found the man lying in the road before Jip got there; that he at once became terrified, thinking him dead or dying, that he would be blamed for it – since his tracks were in the road leading to the man's body.

'And of course it is most likely,' Kling went on, 'that the next thing he'd think of, after covering his own tracks, would be the hiding of the money, either because that also would throw suspicion on him or because he hoped to come later and dig it up after the row had blown over. So one of the first things we have to do before we go away from here is to cover our own tracks, leave everything as we found it and set someone on guard in case the man returns. That, however, I fear there isn't much chance of his doing for a longish time. Still, good detectives leave no loop-holes. We'll get Toby or Swizzle to hide in the bushes here and watch.'

'Then you think we had better leave the money where it is?' I asked.

'Oh, certainly,' said Kling. 'It will be quite safe so long as we have one of the dogs watching. And we will be much more likely to find out things if we don't let on to what we already know. The best detectives always pretend to be as ignorant and as stupid as possible.'

So, thereupon we proceeded to set the stage in the copse just as we found it. Kling, realizing that he probably had an experienced criminal to deal with, took the greatest pains to make sure that we left no trace to show that we had been there. After the earth had been put back into the hole on top of the money-bag he went over all the ground inside the copse slowly and carefully. Wherever the moss or the little under-shrubs had been beaten down by our feet he straightened everything up to wipe out all traces. He even examined the encircling hawthorns lest we might have broken any leaves of left limbs drawn back showing where we had come through.

'I'll bring Swizzle and Toby up here as soon as we get back,' said he, as we struck off across the fields for the gate. 'They can take it in turns to keep watch.'

Before leaving I had taken a rough tracing of the footprint with a pencil and paper, so as to be able to get an idea of which shoes might fit. Of course it wasn't very accurate, but I calculated that with its aid I could cut down the number of shoes I must bring up here to try – even if I did not succeed in making sure at the house.

3

THE SHOE THAT FITTED
THE FOOTPRINT

On our way back, as we approached the Doctor's house, we saw three men descending the steps. The Doctor was standing at the gate at the top watching them. He looked worried and puzzled.

Kling at once shot off and overtook the men. He pretended to be doing nothing in particular; but I noticed by the way he stopped and sniffed in passing them that he was looking for a scent he knew.

'Who are those men, Doctor?' I asked as I joined him and walked up the garden path towards the front door.

'Oh, bother it, Stubbins!' said he rather irritably, 'I don't know and I don't want to know. It is something in connexion with this man we found stunned in the roadway – and the money that was missing. Those two big fellows are plain-clothes men, or private detectives or something of the sort. They wanted to know if I could identify the little man they have with them. He is under arrest, it seems, on suspicion of having done the deed. They asked me when I had seen him last. I never saw him before – thank goodness! I've no idea who he is.'

'But I have, Doctor,' said a voice behind us. And turning we found Matthew Mugg, who had mysteriously appeared from somewhere in the garden and joined us.

'That little bloke was Tobias Wilkes,' he went on. 'I know him well.'

'But I don't,' the Doctor put in hurriedly. 'What on earth are all those shoes on the front steps for?'

'Oh, Kling is doing some investigating on his own

account,' said I. 'He thinks he can find out who struck the man.'

'Good gracious!' cried the Doctor. 'For Pity's sake don't let us have any more mysteries or detective work around here! Haven't we had enough already?'

And leaving us abruptly he fairly ran round the house to the side door to return to his work at which he had been interrupted.

'It'll go hard with poor Tobias,' said Matthew thoughtfully as he watched the Doctor's figure disappear, 'if he can't prove that he was somewhere else that night. His reputation's none too good anyhow. The Doctor's fibbing when he says he never saw him before – unless he has forgotten, convenient-like maybe. Why, he caught Tobias poaching pheasants not over a month ago. That I know, because I was helping Tobias myself at the time – only the Doctor never saw me.'

As I climbed over the pile of old shoes and opened the front door Kling ran up to me.

'Tommy,' said he, 'I'd like to see you alone a moment.'

'Well, Kling,' I said when we were within the hall with the door closed behind us, 'what is it? Was that little fellow the man who hid the money? I saw you sniffing at him as you passed.'

'No, of course he isn't,' said Kling impatiently. 'Those lanky detectives are just plain-clothes fools. This man smells entirely different. The fellow who made that footprint in the copse was the one who hid the money. What I want you to do now, Tommy, is to find the right shoe, if you can, among that pile. I've got to take Toby and Swizzle up to the copse and put them on guard. Blackie and Grab are keen to do it, but I'm afraid of fighting dogs for a job of this kind. They'd go for the man if he came, I know. All we want is small, clever dogs who will follow the fellow and see where he takes the money. So hurry up, will you? Now

91

they've got the wrong man under arrest we've got to get busy.'

Immediately he had gone I set to work with my tracing. Most of the pile of shoes were far too large or too small to leave any doubt. But one pair fitted suspiciously well. Jip was watching me with great interest.

'I remember where we found that pair,' he said. 'It was in a ditch at the bottom of the field where the copse is. Let's follow Kling up there right away and try it in the footprint itself.'

So away we went without further delay.

We found the Dog Detective giving final instructions to his able lieutenants, Toby and Swizzle. He was very carefully repeating to them for the second time the exact place and manner they were to lie hidden and how they were to change guard at intervals. Swizzle, the clown dog, was taking it all as a joke; but Toby, the self-important, was treating it very seriously.

It was a thrilling moment when we laid the shoes over the footprint. It couldn't have fitted better.

'Good!' muttered the Dog Detective. 'That is a big step in the chain of evidence.'

'But, Kling,' I said, 'I don't see how you're going to find the man even now that you are sure that you've got his shoe.'

'No,' said Kling with some condescension, 'having no experience as a criminal investigator, you wouldn't. But you see, I already have my suspicions – and an idea of where to look for my man. In fact, I am pretty certain – by guesswork it is true – of where the man lives. But several men live in the same place. With this shoe I can now tell which of the men it was who hid the money.'

'Good gracious!' I said. 'I had no idea that you had got that far. And where does the man live, might I ask?'

'He lives,' said the Detective Dog, 'at least I strongly

suspect he does – in the same place as the stunned man lives; in the stable hands' quarters up at Squire Jenkins's place. If you will come with me we will now proceed there and continue our investigations.'

I knew Squire Jenkins's place quite well. It was about two miles down the Oxenthorpe Road from the Doctor's house. Here in a fine old Georgian mansion the Squire (who many years ago had been one of the Doctor's patients) kept a large establishment with hunting stables, foxhound kennels and all the other things that in those days went with a big country house.

Around the wide yard behind the main building were the quarters for the grooms and stable hands – of which the Squire kept at least a dozen. This yard was reached by a private road whose gate was always open.

'It is my idea,' said Kling as we reached the gate, 'to drop the shoe in the middle of the yard and then retire to see what happens. We may have luck; we may not. We shall see.'

I hardly expected that any one would object to my going down the private road. But I thought it best to make myself as little noticeable as possible in any case. I knew that no one would be likely to interfere with Kling.

Unchallenged, we got into the yard, where I lounged behind a hay-cart and watched Kling take his shoe out into the middle and drop it. Then he went smelling around just like any stray dog looking for rats.

From time to time various grooms and boys crossed the yard engaged on stable business of one kind or another. All passed the shoe with barely a glance.

But finally a lanky sort of a man with a very disagreeable face came out of a stable door carrying a saddle under his arm. The shoe lay right in his path as he crossed from that corner of the yard to the opposite. As his eye fell on it he gave quite a start. Then, glancing round nervously to make sure no one saw him, he hastily snatched it up from the ground, hid it under the saddle and hurried on. Kling, who had appeared to be examining a gutter the other side of the yard, trotted carelessly across his path, sniffing, before the man disappeared into what seemed to be the harness room.

Then he dawdled around to my side of the hay-cart.

'Did you get a good look at his face, Tommy?' he whispered.

'Yes,' I said, 'I'd know him again anywhere.'

'Good!' whispered the Dog Detective, pretending to scent another rat. 'Then let's be going, shall we?'

4

THE DOG DETECTIVE CONTEMPLATES

WITHOUT further words we left the yard together and made our way down the private road. At the outer gate Jip joined us.

'Well, Kling,' I said, after we had tramped about half a mile in silence, 'what is the next move?'

The Dog Detective, deep in contemplation, made no response.

'Sh!' said Jip. 'Don't disturb him. He's thinking. Sometimes over his knottiest cases he goes into these moods for hours – and days – at a time. He'll speak when he's ready.'

And Jip was quite right. Kling did not speak for another two and a half hours. As soon as he got home he took out one of his old chewing shoes on to the lawn. There the reverie of the great investigator continued, while Jip and I sat around with our mouths open, wondering when he would have done enough thinking – and chewing – to say a little something. In this Gub-Gub came and joined us –

HUGH LOFTING

though Jip was quite firm in making him keep his distance from the meditating detective.

'You've no idea, Tommy,' he whispered to me, 'what a time we've had with that ridiculous hog. He is just determined to follow this case inch by inch. There were moments when we simply had to run to get away from him. You can imagine how much chance two Secret Service Dogs like us would stand of finding out anything with a large grunting pig lumbering along behind us everywhere we went. I managed to shut him into the tool shed once, but he bellowed so loud that the Doctor thought someone was being killed and came running out from his study to see what was the matter – Goodness! Look at Kling. I believe he has found it.'

The Dog Detective had ceased his thoughtful chewing. He was staring, motionless, at the lawn between his feet.

'I wonder,' we heard him mutter to himself at last, 'I wonder. It's possible – quite probable, in fact ... Humph!'

Then suddenly he threw the boot aside, sprang up and disappeared out of the gate leading down the steps on to the road. Jip and I followed him running. So did Gub-Gub – greatly to Jip's annoyance.

In the road outside the gate the great investigator proceeded to run back and forth over the scene of the crime.

'Yes,' he hissed at last, 'it was – I'll bet my last boot it was ... Tommy, our next job is to find a horse ... a horse ... a horse whose off hind-shoe has a bent nail in it.'

'Why?' I asked. 'What do you want him for?'

'Because he is the one who stunned the man,' said Kling.

'Goodness me!' I cried. 'You don't say! Kicked him senseless, do you mean?'

'No, that's the diddling point,' said Kling. 'He *didn't* kick him – of that I'm certain. And yet I'm positive that he is the only one who could have stunned the man. But how the dickens he did it I've yet to find out.'

After a few moments of thought Kling turned back to me.

'Tommy,' said he, 'I think I'll get you to go down to those stables and do a little inquiring among the hands. If you get them chatting they will, maybe, tell you things which I, of course, couldn't learn – that way – unless I talked their language. Meantime I've got some other business in connexion with the case to attend to alone. Oh, and Jip, listen! You might go up to the copse and see if Toby or Swizzle have anything to report.'

Having thus given his assistants their orders, Chief Kling trotted away on his own affairs.

I proceeded at once to the Squire's place, where I strolled

leisurely into the stable yard and tried to engage some of the hands in friendly conversation. It wasn't very difficult. I soon found a lad polishing a snaffle bit who seemed glad to have someone to talk to while he worked. I began by making a few remarks about horses – on which subject he was anxious to show how much he knew. Then I steered the conversation on to the topic of the robbery. The affair had apparently upset the whole establishment quite a little. The man who had been stunned had been the Squire's second head groom. I gathered that he wasn't at all popular with the rest of the stable hands, who were almost pleased that he had been knocked on the head. But the fact that the roads around peaceful Puddleby were evidently not safe for a man to travel alone, was a very different matter and had caused considerable indignation.

'Still,' the boy ended, 'I reckon they got the right party in handcuffs now, sure enough. That fellow Tobias Wilkes will have hard work proving it wasn't him. Squire got two smart detectives down from London, private detectives. He don't trust the police of these parts, Squire don't – thinks they be all fools. But them London fellows didn't take long over making an arrest. And they say they can prove that Wilkes came along that road just about the time that Fred Langley got knocked on the head. And I'll warrant that before long they'll prove he struck the blow and took the money. But he's an artful dodger, that Wilkes. What beats me is how he hid the horse he stole. It's easy to hide a bag of sovereigns, but 'tain't so easy to hide a horse.'

'Oh, was there a horse stolen, too?' I asked, trying hard not to show too much interest.

'Surely there was,' said the lad. 'One of Squire's best hacks; a chestnut mare. She wasn't very young, but she was as fine a mare as you could find in these parts. And she just disappeared after that night as though the earth had swallowed her up. Squire was more upset about her than he was about the money. She wasn't no hunter, but she was his favourite road hack and the cleverest horse, the prettiest pacer, I ever saw. Her name was Tiger Lily.'

Before I left I learned that Langley, the man who had been stunned, was very friendly with the groom who had picked up the shoe. This fellow's name was Smedley. They happened to cross the yard together while I was still talking to the lad. Also I found out that Tiger Lily, the mare, was to have been shod at the Puddleby farriers the morning that she disappeared.

I felt quite proud, as I walked homeward, of my success. I found Kling waiting for me – also Matthew Mugg, who told me he had been making inquiries down in the town and had learned that the general opinion was that Tobias Wilkes would go to jail for a long term.

In a quiet corner of the garden, Kling, Jip and I held a little conference.

'We've got to hurry this thing along more than ever now, Kling,' said I, 'if we are to save Tobias from an unjust sentence.'

'All right, all right,' said Kling, 'I know. The next thing is to find this mare, Tiger Lily. With her story if we can get it from her, and I fancy the Doctor will be able to – the whole case will be complete. The Doctor doesn't want to be mixed in it, I know, but he will hardly refuse when we show him that it will save an innocent man from jail. I found a shoe which I am certain is Tiger Lily's about a mile along the road from where the man was struck down. I know it is hers because it had the bent nail in it which showed in the hoof marks not far from the Doctor's gate. Tracking her might have been possible if we had followed this clue the morning the man was found. But by this time, of course, with all the cart wheels and hoofs going over the road dust in the meantime, that is out of the question. What we need now is a dog with a peculiar gift in scent.'

'How do you mean?' I asked.

'He means,' said Jip, 'a dog with a special nose for horses. Almost any dog is good on man scents. But one who can tell one horse from another by scent is pretty rare. Still, there are such dogs. Listen, Kling! Let's go down to the Home and see what we can do there.'

Together the three of us crossed the big garden to the zoo enclosure. The Home for Crossbred Dogs happened to be just setting to on the evening meal. Jip at once went to the head of the centre table and beat upon it for silence with a ham bone. The chatter and rattling of dishes ceased instantly.

'Members,' said Jip, addressing the dining room in general, 'we have particular and urgent need of a dog with a good nose for horses – one who can follow a single horse scent across the whole length of England, if need be. Is there any member present who thinks he could do that?'

5

TIGER LILY'S TRAIL

ALMOST immediately after Jip ceased speaking a dog left the sideboard buffet where he had been helping himself to sausages and shambled forward through the crowd towards the speaker. He was indeed a sorry-looking animal. He had only one eye; he walked with a limp and seemed quite, quite old. I remembered him at once. He was a mongrel foxhound whom Jip had got into the club long after it was full, by using a lot of influence with the committee and the Doctor.

'Well, Mike,' said Jip, as the veteran came to a halt at the centre table, 'do you think you could do it?'

'I don't think,' said the old dog, swallowing half a sausage which he had brought with him from the sideboard, 'I know I could. I was born in a hunting kennel. But because I wasn't thoroughbred they would never let me run with the pack. Still, I thought my nose was as good as any of 'em – even if I hadn't the speed and the looks. It was a dull life. There was hardly anything for me to do except hang around the stables, where the men used to laugh at me because I was crossbred. The hounds used to make fun of me too. One day I followed the pack anyway, even though the whips tried to beat me off. Of course I couldn't keep up the whole run, but I stuck with 'em for a good six or seven miles. Then I was blown. While I was resting, one of the huntsmen got thrown as he tried to jump a hedge. He was a parson, a nice old fellow who had often been kind to me. His horse took fright and bolted immediately, over the hills and far away. The idea came to me to try and follow this horse and find him for my friend the parson. And after I had got my wind back I up and after him. The whole countryside was, of course, full of the scents of horses. Just the same, I succeeded in singling this one out and trailing him down. I found him grazing fifteen miles away from the place he had spilled his rider. Then I knew I had an extra-ordinary and special scent for horses. And when I began to experiment and train it, I discovered that I could pick one horse out of a hundred with my eyes shut. It is a real gift, but, of course, no use in a fox-hound kennel. To them hunting folk I was just a poor scrub mongrel, good for nothing. Have you got something I can take the scent from for this mare you have lost?'

'Yes,' said Kling, 'we've got a shoe. It hasn't been handled. I left it just where she dropped it.'

'Good!' grunted Mike. 'I'll find her all right. Just wait till I've eaten my sausages. I'll be with you in a minute.'

And turning, the old veteran shambled back to the sideboard to finish his evening meal.

'Listen, Tommy,' said Jip: 'this is likely to be a long run. If we set out on it tonight you had better bring a supply of food and a blanket to sleep in. Goodness only knows how far old Mike may take us.'

'All right,' I said. 'I'll go and get ready. When Mike has finished come and tell me.'

Not wanting to worry the Doctor I merely told him that Jip, Kling and I were going out for a moonlight tramp and might not be home till late the next day. But I borrowed a little money from him in case we should need it. Then, by the time I had made up my bundle of the blanket and sandwiches, the three dogs were already waiting for me in the hall. Poor Gub-Gub tried very hard to join the party, but of course we couldn't take him.

The daylight was just starting to wane as we set out. Kling at once took us to the place where he had found the shoe. Old Mike sniffed at it, grunted and trotted off.

It was a strange journey and a strenuous one. Very soon I saw that with the coming darkness I stood a good chance of getting left behind. For the dogs, eager and long-winded, set a terrible pace at the start – in spite of old Mike's limp. Jip, after I had had to call to them more than once to wait for me, suggested that I tie a string to his collar so that I could keep in touch.

It seemed as though Tiger Lily had been pretty sure of her direction; for the scent hardly ever halted or dawdled around. She had just hit across country, regardless almost of anything. There were places where she had evidently leapt high hedges, forded streams, swum lakes and waded bogs. More than a dozen times I was on the point of telling the dogs that they would have to go on alone to find the trail's end. But the thrill of the chase fascinated me and kept me going through it all.

About midnight I told them that I thought it was time we

all took a rest for I saw that they, too, were pretty well winded. The four of us, therefore, ate a sandwich apiece, rolled ourselves in the blanket under a tree and went fast asleep.

Next morning, after another sandwich all round, we were up and going again through the dewy fields almost before the sun had arisen. Till now I had very little idea of where we were, beyond the guess that we had come in a north-easterly direction away from Puddleby, and had made about twenty miles. And even with the daylight I wasn't much the wiser. The dogs, from their conversation, seemed better acquainted with the neighbourhood than I was. One village which we skirted looked, however, vaguely familiar to me. I asked Jip if he knew the name of it.

'Yes,' said he, 'that's Digby Royal.'

'Digby Royal,' I muttered. 'Curious! The name sounds familiar, too. Can I have been here before?'

And then it dawned on me that I had once on a journey with the Doctor changed coaches at a town of that name. I tried to remember what place we were going to on the journey. But that year the Doctor and I had done a good deal of travelling together about the country in pursuit of ferns, the study of which greatly interested him just then. Still, I thought, I ought to be able to remember.

For some hours, as we trudged along behind Mike, I cudgelled my brains, annoyed with my poor memory.

At last it came to me.

'Jip,' I cried, 'I have an idea of where this trail may lead us.'

'Where?' he called back.

'To the Retired Cab and Wagon Horses' Association,' I said. 'I've just remembered where we were going when we last passed through Digby Royal.'

'By jingo!' muttered Jip. 'That's so. I've gone there many times with the Doctor myself. And this is the way we

HUGH LOFTING

always came. We're now approaching Bentlake. That's where the Doctor and I stopped for lunch last time. Humph! I wonder if you're right.'

'Well,' I said, 'it is certain that the mare would have heard of the Doctor's home for retired horses, living as she does almost next door to John Dolittle's house. And it would be natural enough if she went off by herself, meaning to run away for good, that she would make for that as the best hiding place – in fact the only place where she would be safe from the interference of people.'

Jip said no more, but trotted on after Kling and Mike, wrapped in thought.

The trail artfully went around all the towns as though the mare (I remembered the stable lad's speaking of her extraordinary cleverness) had realized that she would be in danger of being stopped if she passed through streets with no one leading or riding her. On the way we found places where she had evidently lain down to hide from passers-by behind high hedges or in the sheltering refuge of a copse or wood.

I became quite interested in the prospect of meeting this highly intelligent horse. And I began thinking about what Kling had said: that he was sure she had stunned the man — but not by kicking him. Could she have known something about him, disliked him perhaps, and stunned him on purpose to escape. And, above all, how in the world had she done it?

6

TOGGLE'S SILENCE

A s we drew nearer to the district where John Dolittle had established his now well-known Retired Cab and Wagon Horses' Association, Jip and I became surer than ever that my guess had been right. The hills and the farms round about were more familiar territory to me than much of the country nearer home. For I had spent many pleasant days here with the Doctor talking to Beppo and Toggle, the famous old plough horse with green spectacles.

At the main gate to the Rest Farm these two were standing, when we at last came in sight of it, almost as though they had been expecting someone's arrival. They were delighted to see Jip and myself. Of the other dogs, Kling and Mike, they seemed suspicious until we introduced them as part of our party.

Inside the lovely meadows we stretched ourselves beneath the giant elms and ate the last of our sandwiches. We were all weary and dead beat after our long journey.

When I came to question Toggle about the chestnut mare, to my great astonishment he first remained entirely silent. Then, evidently ill at ease, he assured me that no such horse had joined the association. He turned to old Beppo, who also gravely shook his head. Then Kling came up behind me and whispered in my ear:

'They've promised to say nothing. You can see that. Tiger Lily must be here. Old Mike says her scent is all over the place. She's hiding behind a hedge or something.'

'Well, couldn't Mike nose her out?' I whispered back.

'Better not,' said Kling. 'The chances are she would just jump a fence and bolt. And then we'd have another fifty-mile chase to catch up with her again. Let me talk to these old fellows. If the mare is scared it will be best to get them to make her listen to reason.'

Thereupon Kling explained to Beppo and Toggle (who were the president and vice-president of the association) that, first of all, we were quite certain that the mare was here. Secondly, that it was wrong of her to try and stay hidden, because an innocent man was in danger of being sentenced for something he hadn't done; and to clear up the matter it was necessary to tell the police how Langley had been stunned. Also that the Squire, who valued the mare highly, would want to claim her, and the Doctor would get into trouble with him when it became known that she had taken refuge at the Dolittle Rest Farm.

'So you see,' Kling ended, 'it would be far better if you two went to Tiger Lily and persuaded her to come and have a talk with us. Tell her that Tommy will promise to make no attempt to capture her against her will. But we must see her.'

Finally the two old horses seemed to see the sense and fairness of what Kling had proposed. They told us to stay where we were while they drew off a short distance and conferred together in whispers. A little later we saw them disappear behind some hedges and for a while we saw nothing more of them.

'I wouldn't wonder,' Kling whispered, 'if Tiger Lily has been listening all the time somewhere quite near. We've got to be careful how we handle this mare, Tommy. I've a notion she's full of what Bumpo calls temperamentality – skittish and wayward, you know. Look out! Here she comes.'

I don't think I shall ever forget my first sight of Tiger Lily.

For never had I seen a more beautiful, enchanting animal. She suddenly appeared in a gap in the hedge between the two old veterans. It may have been that their aged, broken-down look served to set off her clean, well-groomed, dainty grace. But as she stood there she seemed to me to have something of the almost supernatural about her. From her alert, clever eyes to her neat, slender fetlocks, she was a picture to warm the heart of any man.

It was very evident that though she had consented to come to the parley, she was not placing any great confidence in the promise that she would not be captured. At an easy supple walk she picked her way down the slope in

our direction, but paused a good thirty paces from us and would come no nearer. I noticed those intelligent eyes taking in not only every detail of ourselves but glancing around and beyond to make sure that the way of escape would be easy if any attempt should be made upon her liberty.

As I got up to address her I felt a new and peculiar pride in my knowledge of horse language, since it enabled me to converse with a creature such as this.

'How do you do, Tiger Lily?' I said, smiling to reassure her. 'I am glad that you consented to come and talk with us. Please have no fear. You are not among enemies. We come, as Toggle has no doubt told you, from John Dolittle's house. It is necessary, for the sake of a man who has been wrongly arrested for striking down Fred Langley, that we hear your story of the night and early morning when the thing happened. Won't you please tell us?'

The mare thought for a moment. Then she threw back her shapely head and blew gently through her silky nostrils. The white of her muzzle and a star between her eyes were the only spots that broke the even, glossy chestnut of her coat.

'Yes,' she said at length. 'I'll tell you the whole thing as far as I know it. But I will not come with you. So you can put that out of your minds right away.'

7

HOW THE MARE GOT AWAY

I was disappointed at the mare's words. But before I had a chance to make any comment Kling whispered: 'Don't try to persuade her now. Wait till she has told us her story. Let her get more confidence in us first. Take her easy.'

'This thing goes back,' Tiger Lily began, 'quite a long way – to the time when the road hacks were a much more important part of the Squire's stables than they are now, when people used the roads more and these diabolical railway things which are doing their best to ruin the country-side hadn't been invented. In those days most of the journeys that the Squire and his guests made were done on horseback. But later, when the hunters came to be almost the whole thing at the stables, I and a few hacks that were still kept were put into the stalls at the north end of the yard, and Langley, the second groom, was put in charge of us. Up to that time old George Gibbons, the head groom, had had the management of us, and things were different. The Squire is an easy-going man and a great deal went on in his stables that he never knew of. That fellow Langley is a low-down, cruel, thieving rat. You must excuse my language, but he deserves it, every bit. As soon as he was given sole charge of the hack stables, with the buying of the fodder and everything, he started to cheat the Squire right and left. He cheated us, too. He got the corn chandler to serve us with cheap, mouldy oats, maize with worms in it and bad hay. And all the time he was charging the squire for the best quality, which was what old Gibbons had always got for the stables.

'More than that, he was cruel. He never let the Squire see him, but when no one was around he was always beating us, kicking us and treating us abominably. There was another fellow almost as mean and low as himself, called Smedley.'

(Kling here glanced at me and nodded significantly.)

'Langley made Smedley sort of second-in-command of the hack stables, and when one wasn't knocking us about and swearing at us the other was. Well, one day I noticed these two doing a good deal of whispering and confabbing together and I guessed that they were hatching some plot. All I hoped was that I wasn't going to be in it. But when Langley came and saddled me and took me out of my stall about two o'clock the next morning, I saw that I was going to be in it. It was evident that he meant to steal me – or that's what I feared at the time anyway – and it turned out later I was right. The prospect of being owned and ridden by that horrible man for the rest of my life was too awful for anything. And right away I began to look for a chance to escape from him.'

Kling at this point moved restlessly in the grass as though impatient to hear whether the outcome of Tiger Lily's story fitted in with his own guesswork version of the case.

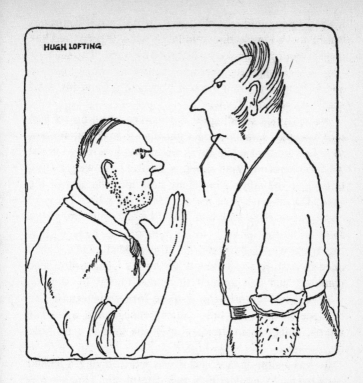

'Well,' the mare went on after a moment, 'Langley led me out through the yard, taking care to walk me always on the soft places so my hoofs would make no noise. Even after he reached the highway he seemed afraid to get up on my back, lest, I suppose, I should go away at a trot and wake someone in the stables. When he had come opposite the Doctor's house he stopped. He had already been looking back a good deal. It seemed to me as though he were expecting someone to join him for he kept muttering words of annoyance. After standing there a little while he started to go back along the road a short way, so that he could see around the bend. He didn't take me with him, fearing again, no doubt, the noise I might make in turning. But he had a long leading rein in his hand. It permitted him to get about five or six yards away from me. I thought of suddenly giving a tug, wrenching the rein out of his hand and bolting. But I saw he had it wound around his wrist and I was afraid to try it.

'He remained standing there a moment with his back to me. It seemed somehow the right time to make an attempt to get away. And while I was wondering how I'd go about it I felt one of my hind shoes, as I shifted my weight from one leg to the other, slip off my hoof into the dust of the road. This at once gave me an idea. From where I stood I could not reach to kick him. But if I could only throw that shoe accurately enough to hit him on the head with it the trick would be done. As it happened, when I was once in pasture with some other horses I had had a shoe come off and had amused them and myself by slipping it on again and throwing it quite long distances. It can be done, if you are only patient enough and a few of the old nails remain standing up in the shoe to get a hold by.

'It was a slim chance, but it was worth trying. I looked back over my shoulder and took careful aim. Langley was standing quite motionless, still looking down the road for his friend who didn't come. I pressed my hoof firmly down on to the shoe so I could pick it up. Then I drew up my right hind foot slowly and shot it out in the direction of Langley's head with all my force. The shoe skimmed through the air whistling and hit him on the head with a thud. He had his cap tilted well back, otherwise it would certainly have killed him. He dropped like a stone and lay still.'

'Then what happened to the shoe?' asked Kling.

'It bounced off his head,' said Tiger Lily, 'and fell a good twenty feet distant. At first I was afraid of being tracked if I

ran away with only three shoes, and I turned and went back for it. I pressed the nails well home into the old holes and managed to keep it on for a few hundred yards. Then, as I was jumping a hedge to get into a field, it came off again, and I saw it was hopeless to try and keep it any longer. So I just hit across country to come here.'

'You never went up close to the man again after he fell?' asked Kling.

'No,' the mare answered. 'I only went around him to get the shoe, which lay off to the side of the road.'

'That's how I knew you hadn't kicked him,' said Kling. 'Your standing backwards tracks were all too far away to reach him with a kick. But you dragged the man a little before you got clear, did you not?'

Tiger Lily's bright eyes opened wide as she looked at this mysterious dog who seemed to know everything.

'Yes,' she said. 'The leading rein was wound so tight about his wrist I couldn't get free. But I only dragged him a couple of feet before it slipped away. How on earth did you know?'

'Pshaw!' said Kling, tossing his head. 'The track where he had been drawn along in the dust was as plain as a pikestaff. Now tell us, did you see anything of the man Smedley that night – or rather morning?'

'Yes,' said Tiger Lily. 'I can just say that I saw him. When I went back for the shoe I got a glimpse of him hurrying down the road. I'm pretty certain it was he. But, of course, I didn't wait till he came up. In fact, that's why I jumped the hedge. I didn't want anyone to see me and follow me ... That is all of my story. Now I think I'll be going.'

'Oh, but just a minute, Tiger Lily,' said I. 'Don't you see that your staying here is likely to make things very awkward for Doctor Dolittle? If you came back with us, it –'

'I am *not* coming back with you,' the mare quickly interrupted, getting ready to bolt. 'Nothing in the world would induce me to.'

'Don't get her scared,' whispered Kling. 'All right,' he said aloud, turning to the mare again. 'We are not going to force you. But listen: if John Dolittle comes here will you speak with him?'

'Oh, certainly,' said Tiger Lily – 'of course.'

'Very good then,' said Kling. 'Thank you very much for you information. Let us be going, Tommy.'

And as soon as we had said good-bye to Toggle and Beppo we made our way out through the main gate.

8

NEWS FROM TOBY

'Humph!' said I as we started off along the road. 'Just the same, we didn't do a bad night's work. We found the mare and we got her story ... Poor old Doctor! It looks as though we shall have to drag him into it after all. Do you think she will come – even with him, Kling?'

'Oh, of course,' said the Detective Dog. 'All her panic is over those two low fellows, Langley and Smedley. I don't blame her myself. But, after all, she doesn't know us, and she is in a sort of hysterical state. But once the Doctor guarantees her that she won't have to have anything to do with those two, she'll come all right. I learned from some of the dogs around the stable yard that the Squire himself is very kind to his animals. And you heard her tell us that she was happy there until that horrible Langley got put in charge.'

'I wonder what is the quickest way we can get back,' said Jip. 'Old Tobias Wilkes is the one that I'm thinking of. I wish we had something faster than our legs to carry us.'

'Look here,' I said. 'I got a little money from the Doctor before I left. Let's hurry on to Digby Royal and see if we can't catch a coach from there. I think I have enough for the fare.'

So, putting our best foot forward, we reached Digby Royal before noon. Luckily a coach was leaving at half-past one. After asking the cost of the journey I found that I had enough to buy us all a light lunch in addition – of which we were all more than glad.

We got back to Puddleby about tea time. Dab-Dab was very angry with us for not letting her know we would be away so long; and Gub-Gub was consumed with interest to know where we had been, what we had done and how much we had found out.

I waited till tea was over before I tackled John Dolittle on the subject of his going to interview Tiger Lily.

'You're the only one who can bring her back, Doctor.' I said, after I had outlined the situation to him. 'There's no doubt about that. And I'm really afraid that if the Squire's detectives get combing over the country they will find out where she's hiding and then they'll be after you. It would be best, I think, if you went and saw her right away and tried to make her listen to reason.'

The poor Doctor, who was in the midst of a very important treatise on the subject of moths, looked up at me wearily, but said nothing.

'And besides,' I added, 'we need you to get Wilkes out of this. He's in a very serious situation.'

Well, the Doctor finally saw, of course, that if he didn't take a hand in it, it was going to be a very complicated business for all concerned, and a decidedly grave one for Tobias Wilkes. When I had finished he sent me for Kling, and asked the Detective Dog to tell him his version of the story from beginning to end. After which he sat silent for a little, thinking.

While we were still waiting for him to speak we heard a pattering of paws on the gravel outside the study window and suddenly Toby sprang up on to the sill.

'Kling!' he cried. 'Someone came back after the money while I was on the watch. That fellow Smedley – from Squire Jenkins's place.'

'Well, did you trail him?' asked the Detective Dog.

'Yes,' said Toby. 'And he came down the Oxenthorpe Road. I think he's going into Puddleby on foot. He has only

just gone by our gate. But you'll have to hurry if you want to catch him.'

In a moment the Doctor and I were out in the front garden and leaping down the steps. After us came not only Kling, Toby and Jip, but Blackie, the retriever, and Grab, the bulldog, as well. At a distance of not more than a couple of hundred yards from the gate we saw the figure of a man hurrying along towards the town as fast as he could go. He looked over his shoulder, and seeing us, put on even more speed – indeed he seemed about to break into a run.

'Go after him, Blackie,' said the Doctor quietly. 'Don't

hurt him, but just get ahead of him and keep him where he is till we can catch up.'

Blackie, followed by Grab and Jip, shot after the hurrying figure, which they promptly surrounded and brought to a standstill.

At first when the Doctor came up and spoke to him, Smedley's manner was a mixture of fear and brazenness. But after it had been explained to him that his partnership with Langley and all the other details of the case were well known to us, he was just terrified and nothing more. He started to excuse himself for his part of it, trying to throw the entire blame upon Langley. But the Doctor cut him short.

'There is only one thing that can save you from a heavy sentence,' said he. 'And that is that you do exactly as I tell you. To begin with, give me the money.'

Smedley was evidently for a moment going to deny that he had it. But something about the Doctor's determined look and the fact that he already seemed to know everything, made him realize that that would be useless. Shamefacedly he brought the linen bag out of his pocket and handed it to the Doctor.

'The next thing,' said John Dolittle, 'go and get Langley and bring him to my house – that one there, with the steps leading up to it. If your friend should be unwilling to come just explain to him that it will cost him his liberty as well as yours. We have both your descriptions. You could not get far. If the two of you are not at my house within half an hour I will inform the police of all that I know.'

9

TIGER LILY'S RETURN

As a precaution Kling dispatched his able lieutenant Toby to shadow Smedley when he left the Doctor's house. But this turned out to be unnecessary. Apparently Langley was quickly persuaded that it was wiser to fall in with the Doctor's orders than to try to get away, for less than twenty minutes later we saw the two men coming up the garden path. I opened the front door myself and took them at once to the Doctor's study.

Kling and I were the only others present at the interview. John Dolittle did not take long over it. In as few words as possible he showed them that the whole truth of the case was in his possession and what he now proposed to do.

'Much will depend,' he ended, 'on whether the Squire decides to drop the case or not. I am hoping for your sakes – though you richly deserve punishment – that I can persuade him to go no further with the matter of the money and the horse are restored to him. What I should recommend you to do is to go away from this district altogether and make a new start. And remember, if at any time you are tempted to go in for this sort of crooked game again, that your faces are well known to me and several witnesses here.'

The two men, who had been very plainly terrified of what the Doctor might do, were quite overjoyed at this permission to escape. As a matter of fact, they wasted no time over it, but got out that same evening and were never seen again in the neighbourhood of Puddleby.

The Doctor's interview with the Squire was somewhat more difficult. Indeed, if the old Squire had not known

John Dolittle so well it is doubtful if it would have been successful at all. But finally, after the doctor had talked to him for quite a while, he agreed to withdraw his detectives from the case. And as it was they who had accused Tobias Wilkes, that was the end of that charge and Wilkes was released.

'And if, Squire,' said the Doctor as he was leaving, 'you should find that one, or perhaps two, of your stable hands suddenly depart from your employ, you will not make any attempt to trace them up, eh?'

At this the Squire looked sharply at his old friend and pondered a moment before answering. Finally he laughed.

'All right, Doctor,' said he. 'You know more than you're letting on to, I reckon. No, I'll go no further with the business. I've come out of it pretty well, thanks to you. I've got the money back, and if you can find Tiger Lily for me I'll be glad enough to call it quits. Seems to me you've been to a peck of trouble on my account. Maybe the day will come when I can do something for you.'

'The job now, Stubbins,' said the Doctor as we came away from the Squire's house, 'is to tackle Tiger Lily. I hope she will not be unreasonable. If she is, there will be nothing left but to buy her from the Squire and leave her at the Rest Farm. And goodness only knows how much that will cost ... Well, we shall see.'

The Doctor set out for the Rest Farm the following day and Kling and I accompanied him.

As a matter of fact, I was half hoping that the mare would refuse to return, because then there might be a possibility, when she had been bought by the Doctor, that I would sometimes get a ride on her. I felt it must be great fun to ride a horse as clever as Tiger Lily.

As usual, a tremendous fuss was made over John Dolittle by all the members of the association when he arrived at the gate. And he was kept busy answering questions for a good half-hour before he had a chance to bring forward the matter of his own business.

One of the horses went off and brought Tiger Lily, who was still keeping to the secluded parts of the farm for fear any people passing on the road might recognize her. The difference between her manner with John Dolittle and that in which she had received me and Kling the other day was very noticeable. She seemed genuinely glad to see him and came up to where he stood with all the confidence in the world.

Then very gently, just as though he were chatting about the weather or anything, he told her she need have no fear about going back because the two men she disliked had already left the Squire's employment, never to return. He promised her, moreover, that if the groom that took Langley's place wasn't to her liking, he himself would speak of it to the Squire, who would surely see that her complaints were attended to.

She listened thoughtfully and at the end she said:

'All right, Doctor, I'll come. But I want you to promise me as well that when my riding days are over you will buy me from the Squire and let me come back here.'

'Certainly,' said the Doctor. 'I feel pretty sure that the Squire will consent to that. Now, did you bring a saddle with you?'

'Yes,' said she. 'But I rubbed it off against the scratching-post. I had to bite through the girths to do it. But I dare say you can patch it up for one journey.'

To my great delight, the Doctor, who knew that I was crazy to ride the beautiful mare, suggested that I take her back while he and the dogs went by coach. Tiger Lily very graciously consented to this also – though she told me before the journey was over that I was about the worst horseman she had ever travelled under. Just the same, it was the

HUGH LOFTING

grandest ride I ever had; and I learned more from her remarks on the way about 'good hands' and a firm seat than I had ever known before.

When we were seated at supper that night (Dab-Dab had, among other things for us, a late crop of very wonderful green peas) Gub-Gub as usual demanded that we give an account of our day's doings. We told him that Tiger Lily had been brought back and restored to the Squire.

'But what about Tobias Wilkes?' he asked.

'Oh, I went down to the police station,' said the Doctor, 'with the Squire himself. Wilkes is already released from custody.'

'Custardy!' grunted Gub-Gub, bringing his nose up out of a plate of peas. 'Who's custardy?'

'No, it's nothing to do with custard,' said Jip contemptuously. 'The Doctor means that he is already released from jail. Your mind is just a food mind – as has been remarked before.'

'Well, there are worse kinds of minds than food minds,' said Gub-Gub. 'Goodness! I wish I had brought my food spectacles to supper with me. These peas are so small I can hardly see them. Hump! So Wilkes is released and the mare returned. Then I suppose that's the end of the Mystery of the Stunned Man. Kling is a fine detective and it was an elegant mystery. I wonder what the next one will be?'

'There are not going to be any more,' said the Doctor quickly.

'I should think not indeed!' snorted Dab-Dab, glowering indignantly upon Gub-Gub.

'After all a little mystery goes a long way,' put in Chee-Chee, the monkey.

'In Africa,' said Polynesia, 'there was a good deal too much mystery. On the other hand, it was a wonderful climate. I don't like the way that wind is wailing in the chimney. Heigh, ho! I suppose the summer's over already and the blithery, shivery time is beginning. I think I'll borrow one of the Doctor's socks and make a sweater out of it.'

'But if we're not allowed to have any more mysteries and detective cases,' said Gub-Gub, 'what are we going to do for amusement in the long winter evenings? The Doctor is always too busy now to tell us stories round the fire.'

'What are the animals talking about, Tommy?' asked Bumpo.

'The Doctor was just telling Gub-Gub that we'd had enough of mysteries and detective work,' said I.

'Oh, deciduously so,' said Bumpo, biting into an enormous slab of bread and treacle. 'I never cared for an atmos-mear of mystery.'

'Listen, Stubbins,' said the Doctor, 'if you have finished I think we had better go over to the Home for Crossbred Dogs right away and speak to Kling before he gets started on a new problem of some kind. I really can't have any more interruptions. I am dreadfully behindhand with my book on moths.'

'So am I – on my book,' said Gub-Gub, pushing his plate forward for more peas.

'Your book!' screeched Too-Too. 'What book are you writing, for pity's sake?'

'*The History of Food*,' said Gub-Gub quietly – 'a most important work. It's nearly done. I only have seven more volumes.'

THE CRESTED SCREAMERS

I

REGENT'S PARK

WHEN Doctor Dolittle was preparing his Canary Opera to be shown in London he went to the Zoo in search of bird-singers and bird-dancers for the choruses. Cheapside, the London sparrow, and Becky, his wife, went along to help. Gub-Gub, the pig, who assisted the Doctor in the production of the show, was eager to be in on the casting.

'Can I go to the Zoo?' he asked.

'You can *not*,' snapped Cheapside. 'Do you want to get us arrested? 'Ow far do you think the Doc would get with a full-sized porker a'followin' 'im through the crowd?'

So, much to poor Gub-Gub's disappointment at again being left behind, the Doctor finally set out with only the sparrows for company.

''Ow long is it since you was at the Zoo, Doctor?' asked Cheapside when, after forty minutes' walk, they were beginning to approach the neighbourhood of Regent's Park.

'Oh, my!' said John Dolittle, 'it must be – let me see – it must be more than two years now, Cheapside, since I was there.'

'Humph!' said the sparrow with a knowing air. 'I reckon you'll find it changed considerable. Much bigger. But you'll 'ave a better chance to see the kind of thing you want. The collection of birds 'ere is the best in Europe now.'

'How do you know?' asked the Doctor.

'Oh, I've been around all the Zoological Gardens on the Continent,' said Cheapside very grandly. 'You know we used to live in Regent's Park, as I told you. And Becky, 'ere, has been pestering me ever since we left to go back there. But I always told 'er you can't beat St Paul's. It's more central. One time she was at me so hard that I told 'er I'd take 'er on a trip around the Zoos of Europe – just to pacify 'er like. But when she come back she was more in love with Regent's Park than ever.'

'What countries did you visit?' asked the Doctor.

'Pretty near all of 'em,' sighed Cheapside. 'We did a grand tour. But we was both glad to get back to London. Still, some of them furrin cities wasn't so bad. They've got an awful big Zoo in 'Amburg and another in Hantwerp. But I didn't think much of them. I liked Paris. They've got a nice place there they call the Jardong day Plonks – fine lot of parrots and macaws. Noisy things. But the park I liked best in Paris was the Twiddle-didee Gardens, near the Lufer Palace. There's an old feller there – nobody knows 'ow old 'e is – who makes a speciality of feedin' the sparrers. 'E's done it for years. 'As 'is picture took regular, 'oldin' up 'is 'and with crumbs, and sparrers settling all over 'im. 'Course while me and Becky was in Paris, we got most of the crumbs. Them French sparrers ain't much good at fightin'. Some of them is so polite with their "After you, sirs," that I wonder they don't starve to death. I liked Paris pretty good. Becky 'ere said she thought it was a kind of frivolous place. From there we went on to Geneva, Switzerland – you know, where the cuckoo-clocks come from. There they've got a park about the size of a back yard, what they calls the Jardong Onglays – that's the parley-voo for the English Garden. The cheek of 'em! There's nothing English about it. Ain't even got dandelions in it. From there we went on to Rome, Barcelona, Madrid and all the rest. We did a regular tour. But we was both glad to get back to dear old London.'

'Yes,' said Becky, 'and you made straight for St Paul's and settled down in the noisiest part of the city. That's all that travel did for you. Instead of broadening your mind, it made you narrower than ever. Who would want to make his home in the most crowded corner of the city – right on top of the Royal Exchange – when there's Regent Park and all that fine open country to live in?'

'Oh, well,' said Cheapside, 'don't let's 'ave that old argument all over again. 'Ere we are, comin' to the Park now. Most of the leaves is fallen. But it's nice any time of year.'

As John Dolittle entered at the gates of Regent's Park he had to admit that this was indeed, as Mrs Cheapside had said, an ideal place for a city sparrow to make his home. Big elms, horse chestnuts and all manner of other trees rose from the wide greenswards. Fine, well-kept flower beds bordered the walks. Snug, secluded shrubberies, fenced off from the public, offered safe and quiet nesting thickets. Nor was it by any means too countrified for a city-bred bird. Human company, from which the house sparrow seldom stays far away, was here in plenty. Nursemaids, pushing perambulators and leading children, were everywhere. And through this park all the visitors to the Zoological Gardens had to pass. There were open-air restaurants, where families out for the day could take their meals at little tables beneath the big elms. The plump, well-fed sparrows gobbling up the crumbs showed that no bird need starve in this part of London.

'Yes, Doctor,' said Cheapside, when John Dolittle called his attention to this, 'but for grub I'm still better off in the city proper. For good kitchen service the Café de Gutter 'as got this beaten easy.'

'The Café de *what*?' asked the Doctor.

'The Café de Gutter.' Cheapside repeated. 'You know – the all-night coffee stall – lunch wagons. 'Ere in the park folks only 'old picnics in the summer. Cold, perishin' winter days, when a sparrer is really 'ard up for a bite, you can't get anything 'ere. Oh, when it's warm, yes, you could choke a helephant to death on all the 'ard-boiled heggs and sandwich scraps a'blossomin' on the lawns. But not in winter – hoh, no indeed! Folks don't come out lookin' at the pretty polar bears when there's an east wind blowin'. But the coffee stall, that's open all night. Cabbies, bobbies, street washers, market gardeners coming up to the counter regular every five minutes, dribblin' their crumbs down on to the pavement. I know this bloomin' city back to front, I do. And I says, to keep the wolf from the door – in all weathers, mind you – roost me next to the Café de Gutter.'

'Well, you could live here in summer,' said his wife, 'and go back to the cathedral for the winter, couldn't you? That's what I've been asking you to do for the last three years and more. It's better for the children, too – to be brought up in this quiet, restful park, instead of goin' to sleep every night to the racket of the cab wheels and the yelling of the newspaper boys.'

'That's all right, Becky,' said Cheapside. 'But, just the same, our youngsters 'ave all thriven on it. When some of 'em was peevish and wanted special dainty foods there wasn't nothing you'd mention that I couldn't get you at a moment's notice. You remember them hasparagus tips I pinched from the Covent Garden Market at four o'clock in the mornin', when Bertie was 'avin' spasms in 'is stummick? Huh! Like to know where you'd get such dainties anywhere else in a hemergency. No, take it all round, Becky, you can't beat St Paul's. It's so central.'

2

CHEAPSIDE TELLS A STORY

E V E N before they reached the entrance to the Zoo enclosure John Dolittle was greeted by several animals that inhabited the park in a free, wild state. Portly wood pigeons flew down from the great elms, cooed good day and told him they were glad to see him in the city. Squirrels, full of cheeky energy, came bounding out from under rhododendron bushes and bade him welcome. For these creatures Cheapside, proud as Punch to be the great man's guide, showed the most utter contempt.

'All squirrels are thieves – natural pickpockets,' he said. 'And all wood pigeons are gluttons. When Becky and me lived here regular it took us all our time to get a decent meal when them fellers were around.'

At the entrance to the Zoo the Doctor paid his admission at a little window.

'You don't 'ave to pay for us, Doc,' chuckled Cheapside. 'We fly in over the top. And anyway we're entitled to season tickets because we used to be residents 'ere.'

'You ought to be members of the Royal Zoological Society,' laughed the Doctor.

'Well, I reckon we know as much natural 'istory as some members I could mention,' said Cheapside.

Inside, the first thing the Doctor noticed was that some of the pens were being painted and many evidently just done.

'Oh, it's a good Zoo, this,' said Cheapside, gazing round with pride. 'They always keep it spick and span. The paint smells awful while it's drying. But this Zoo is the cleanest, best kept in the world.'

In a big space near the bandstand there was a restaurant.

And the Doctor thought that before starting on his tour of inspection he would like a cup of tea. So he sat down at one of the small tables and was presently served by a waitress. Becky and Cheapside shared the Doctor's meal (much to the envy of the other Zoo sparrows who gathered around) by standing beside his teacup and gobbling the cake crumbs that fell from the great man's plate.

'Over there,' said Cheapside, 'on t'other side of the bandstand you 'ave our prize exhibit.'

'It looks to me like another tea garden,' said the Doctor, gazing across the clearing.

'That's what it is,' said the sparrow. 'It's the members' enclosure. See the sign: *For members only*. It's for members of the Royal Zoological Society. That's for fear you might think it was for members of the monkey 'ouse. That old scarecrow in the 'igh black 'at, that's Sir William Gigglebeck, F.R.Z.S. 'E knows less about natural 'istory than any man living. But 'e's always on show 'ere, drinking 'is tea in the members' enclosure. Did you ever see such a face? I wonder the children don't throw 'im peanuts. Look at 'im a' gazin' at us through 'is monocle, super-silly-ass like. 'E's wonderin' who you are, Doc. That's a joke, isn't it? 'Im what don't know one end of an animal from another, puttin' on airs with you, the greatest naturalist the world ever saw! Yes, that's a good one, that is.'

'What is that large cage next door to the enclosure?' asked the Doctor, pouring out a second cup of tea.

'Oh, that's the Crested Screamers' Aviary,' said Cheapside. 'Good fellows, they are, Screamers. All birds like 'em. From time beyond recollection they've protected smaller birds from harm – when they was wild, that is. That's why I used to get currants for 'em when I lived 'ere. They love 'em.'

'Currants?' said the Doctor. 'Where did you get them?'

'I used to pick them out of the members' buns,' said

Cheapside, 'over at the tea house next door. Yes, old William Gigglebeak 'ad to go without currants in 'is bun when I lived 'ere. They all went to the Screamers. It's funny, that saved my life once – doing them a good turn.'

'How was that?' asked the Doctor.

'It's a long story,' said Becky, gobbling a piece of bread which John Dolittle had given her.

'Well, I should like to hear it,' said the Doctor. 'What you tell me of the Screamers protecting all other birds interests me. Go ahead, Cheapside. We have a long walk before us to get round the whole collection. And I'll be glad of another ten minutes' rest.'

'Well,' Cheapside began, 'it was about a month after I came to live 'ere that the Crested Screamers were first brought to the Zoo. I remember their arrival well. There was considerable excitement in the bird collection all around, because, of course, we knew their reputation. And me, along with half a dozen other sparrows what made the Zoo their home, goes to call on the newcomers. They seemed kind of mopey and down-in-the-mouth, 'cause they'd only just been captured not so long ago. So we tried our best to make 'em feel they were among friends. And the first thing I asks 'em is what they like best in the food line. They wasn't very interested, to begin with. But presently, when a few of 'em had worked up an appetite, they admits that their greatest delicacy was currants, dried currants.

'"All right," I says, "I'll have to see what can be done," and off I flits on a sort of foragin' expedition. I goes to the ordinary restaurant and tea shops. Then I visits the old feller who keeps the sweetmeat stall – you know, sells chocolates and goodies for the children. But I don't find no currants – pretty much everything else in the food line, but no currants. So then Becky says to me, she says: "'Ow about the Members' Enclosure? They 'ave tea there continual. Let's go and see if we can't get some currants there."

'So we trundles off together to inspect the Members' menoo. Well, we was just disgusted. They kept nothing but seed cake. Seems old Gigglebeak was very partial to it. Then I puts on my thinking cap. And after considerin' heavy for a while I says to Becky, I says, "We've got to fix it so they keep currant buns or currant cake in the Members' Tea House."

'"Yes," she says, "But 'ow are you goin' to manage it?"

'"The rats," I says. "Let's go and see the rats."'

3

CURRANTS FOR THE SCREAMERS

'THEN we goes to the back door of the house kitchen and 'angs around there till an old rat comes chasing 'isself out of a hole next the cellar winder.

' "Look 'ere," I says, grabbin' 'im by the tail. "I would 'ave words with you. Them Crested Screamers what came in last night is a special kind of bird what always protects smaller birds in the wild state. It's up to us to see that they're kept comfortable when they're down on their luck and in captivity, see? Now, they only keep seed cake 'ere for the Members. What we want you to do is to pinch the seed cake or spoil it in some way – you have the run of the larder and you know where it's kept, and all that – and continue pinchin' it or spoilin' it till they give up keeping seed cake and take currant buns, see?"

' "Oh, no," 'e says, wiggling 'is whiskers virtuous-like, "I don't see 'ow I can do that."

' "Well," I says, "you jolly well find out a way – and quick. It's up to all us fellers that makes our home in the Zoo 'ere to see that the Screamers are treated right in return for what they've done for the smaller fellers when they was free. And if you don't fall in with my ideas I'll tell every bloomin' animal in the Zoo to treat you as a foreign henemy. You live on the scraps fed to the exhibits, same as we do. Well, take my word for it, you'll 'ave a very thin time if you don't do as I say. Now, get all your friends on the job and hop about it."

'Them rats,' Cheapside continued, 'managed it all right. In fact, they started out by doing it too well, you might say. What do you think they did? The oldest of 'em – oh, an artful old dodger, 'e was – the one I'd spoken to, 'e goes and spills a bottle of rat poison on the seed cake. 'E'd been at the game so long, dodging traps and ferrets and all the other inventions for killin' rats, that 'e knew the smell – even with a cold in 'is 'ead – of every rat poison on the market. And in all 'is cunnin' ways 'e 'ad instructed the other rats that lived under the tea house. Well, 'e knew where the bottle of poison was kept and after I left 'im 'e goes and spills it all over the seed cake what was set out in the pantry for tomorrow's tea.'

Cheapside paused a moment, grinning thoughtfully.

'You never saw such an 'ow-d'ye-do,' he chuckled presently. 'That afternoon about four o'clock me and Becky 'ears a great commotion over at the Members' Enclosure. We 'ops across to see what it was all about, and there was Sir William Gigglebeak being carried off to 'ospital with a terrible pain in 'is stummick. You know, the funny part of it was that that particular rat poison was Sir William's hin-vention – 'is only contribution to the science of natural 'istory, in fact. And 'e was very proud of it. But 'is nose wasn't scientific enough to catch the smell of it on the seed cake. So I says to Becky, I says, " 'E ought to rechristen 'is mixture *Members' Poison* and mark the poison *For Members only* like the sign on the tea-house."

' "But lor bless me!" she says, "this is serious, you know. We can't 'ave the Members killed off like this. You better go and see that rat again and tell 'im to think of something else."

' "All right," I says. "Though I don't fancy most of the Members would be any great loss to natural 'istory. Still, maybe you're right."

'So we goes round to the tea house kitchen and tells our friend 'is methods, while they was thorough, was a bit dras-tic, and 'e must find some other way to cure the Members'

taste for seed cake. But as a matter of fact there wasn't no
need for no further conspiring' on our part. Old William
Gigglebeak got well again after about two weeks of colic;
and when 'e showed up again at the Enclosure the first
order 'e gave was that 'e didn't want to see no more seed
cake in the tea house, never no more. Then they ordered in
a lot of currant buns and plum cakes for the Members' tea;
and we was all right. Me and Becky and a dozen of our pals
used to spend two hours every afternoon picking up currants from under the chairs and even nicking them out of
the buns on the tables when no one was lookin'. And we
put our collection together every evening and took 'em

across to the Crested Screamers and dribbled 'em in through the wire netting on the top of their cage.'

4

CHEAPSIDE HAS A NARROW ESCAPE

'WELL, even though they was in captivity, the Screamers still did one small bird a good turn. And that was me. We 'ad a family of young ones in the nest and Becky 'ere used to ask me to go and get 'er suet every once in a while to feed 'em. You know young birds need a certain amount of meat. And sometimes I would get bits of fat out of the lions' den when they was sleeping after a heavy meal; and sometimes I'd get it other places. And among these places was the Owl House. In those days the Owl House stood next to the Screamers' Aviary, on the other side of the Members' Enclosure. It was a low shed, with the usual runway at the back, covered with wire nettin'; and it was divided into six compartments. In the centre was the Great Horned Owl – an ugly old sinner if ever there was one! "Our Mr Grouch" we used to call 'im. Never had a good word to say to nobody.

'Our Mr Grouch, the Great Horned Owl,' Cheapside went on, 'didn't like me poppin' into 'is cage for bits of meat – said so more than once and warned me to keep out of 'is territory if I didn't want me bloomin' 'ead bit off. But, as 'e usually slept on 'is perch most of the day, I used to slip through a tear in the netting and help meself without askin' 'is permission.

'One day Becky sent me out to get some suet, and after huntin' around several cages and pens without success I says to meself, I says, "I'll go and try me luck in Mr Owl's dinin' room." And off I goes. Well, it was a fine afternoon

136

and our Mr Grouch was snoozin' on 'is perch, dead to the world. So I pops in through the rent in the nettin' and starts foragin' around quiet-like. I 'adn't been there more than a minute or two before a keeper comes in. And I slips behind the door, so I won't be seen. The keeper sweeps the place up a bit, and then, as luck would 'ave it, before he goes out he stands a heavy iron plate, what was used for the owl's meat, right over the hole in the nettin' what I'd been using as a door to get in and out by.

'Mr Grouch had hardly woke up for the keeper's coming. And as soon as the coast was clear I starts hunting not for suet, but for a way to get out. The iron plate was much too heavy for me to move, so I searches the netting all over to see if I can find another hole to get through. I knew, of course, that, once Mr Owl wakes, when the darkness comes, it was all over with me. 'E'd warned me to keep out. And in the dark, against his eyes and quick flight, I wouldn't stand a chance. 'E'd just eat me. That was all there was to it. So you can bet I searched the nettin' pretty thorough. But not one blessed place could I find where a sparrow could get through.

' "Well," I thought, "my only 'ope is to 'ide somewhere till daylight. Then he'll go to sleep again and I may slip out when the keeper comes in with 'is breakfast."

'So I tucks myself away in the corner behind 'is drinking bowl, says a prayer and 'opes for the best — wonderin' what Becky's thinking when I don't come back with the suet. Darkness begins to come on and Mr Owl stretches 'isself and wakes up. The first thing he does is sniff!

' "Oh Lord!" I thinks to meself. " 'E smells me already!"

'And, sure enough, 'e starts right away 'unting around every corner of his place, just as though he knew for certain I was there. My fevvers stood straight up on the top of me 'ead with fright. At last 'e comes to the drinking bowl,

HUGH LOFTING

peers behind it with those great eyes of 'is, glowin' like
lamps in the dark, and sees me!

'"Now I've got you, you little devil!" 'e says. And he
jumps for me. I shoots up into the air. And then a grand
chase began all around the cage.

'"It's no use," I keeps sayin' to meself. "'E's bound to get
me in the end. 'Is speed's twice as good as mine."

'But I'd forgotten my friends, the Crested Screamers,
next door. They'd seen me go into the Owl House, and they
'adn't seen me come out. And when they 'ears the two of us
flutterin' around they guessed what was wrong. And suddenly the whole lot of 'em – a dozen there was – starts

screaming at the top of their voices. And the watchman, thinkin' some animal has got loose, comes rushin' out with a lantern and goes all along the aviaries, to find out what the matter was. Then, seeing the Great Horned Owl a' thrashin' around the cage after something in the dark, he opens the door. And before you could say Jack Robinson I was on the outside, lookin' in, makin' faces at Mr Grouch and thankin' my lucky stars and the Crested Screamers.'

'My gracious!' said the Doctor. 'You had a narrow escape. But all's well that ends well.'

'That's Shaker-spear – all's well wot ends well – ain't it, Doc?' asked Cheapside.

'Yes,' laughed the Doctor. 'Shakespeare said it first. It's a most useful quotation – fits a lot of situations. Shall we get on with the search?'

'Righto!' said the sparrow. 'Come on, Becky, let's show the Doctor the Owls. They'd make a roarin' good endin' for the first act of 'is opera. Sort of a *'Oo, 'Oo, 'OO's the Crew, Wot Sails the Bloomin' Bloo*, chorus.'

THE GREEN-BREASTED MARTINS

I

THE LAND OF THE GAMBIA GOO-GOOS

MANY years ago Doctor Dolittle went to Africa to cure the monkeys who were sick. The part of the country where he landed was called the Land of the Jolliginki and the King of the Jolliginki didn't like strangers in his lands. So he threw the Doctor and his family into jail. Prince Bumpo, the King's son, was kind-hearted and secretly let the Doctor and his animal family escape. They made a hasty departure from the land without carefully checking their provisions.

Poor Bumpo, who knew little about the needs of a sailing voyage – having lived on land all his life – had gone into the King's cellars and, in the dark, snatched any boxes that were near at hand and popped them into the Doctor's ship.

Dab-Dab, the duck, who was chief cook on the voyage, was horrified when she opened box after box and found nothing but yams – a sort of sweet potato.

'Yams! Yams!' she complained. 'How can I prepare a decent meal with nothing but yams!'

'Heavens preserve us!' groaned Gub Gub, the pig. 'But I know that the King ate parnsips as well because I smelt them when those horrible soldiers were dragging us through the palace jail. That stupid Bumpo! Why didn't he look in the boxes? I'll starve before I'll eat this stuff!'

'Oh, be quiet!' snapped Dab-Dab. 'You wouldn't starve if you didn't eat until you got home! There's enough fat on your ribs to feed you for a month!'

'Now, now, Dab-Dab,' said the Doctor. 'It's natural for pigs to be fat. How do you cook yams?'

'I wouldn't know!' said Dab-Dab in a huff.

'It's quite easy,' said the pushmi-pullyu. 'You peel the yams, cut them up and then fry them in the palm oil. That's what is called palm oil chop, the commonest dish of the black people. I'll show you how it's done.'

'Thank you,' said the Doctor. 'It's lucky we had you with us – without somebody who knew African cooking we might have starved.'

'What's this stuff?' asked Jip, the dog, who was undoing one of the other boxes. 'It smells horrible!'

'Dried locusts,' said the pushmi-pullyu. 'They are a kind of large grasshopper. You fry them, too. They're quite good.'

'Pooh! Insects!' snorted Jip.

Everybody was very hungry. And after the pushmi-pullyu had shown them in the ship's kitchen how to prepare palm oil chop they all tried it and were surprised to find that it was not half bad. The grasshoppers, however, of which there was a great quantity in the hold, they refused to touch.

But after a few days having the same dish for breakfast, lunch and supper began to get tiresome. Now, for the first part of the journey home the ship kept sailing along northward, still in sight of the coast of Africa. And one night, after supper, when they were all feeling more than usually tired of palm oil chop, the Doctor said:

'I think it would be a good idea, as soon as we have got safely past the Kingdom of Jolliginki, if we stopped and went ashore somewhere and got a few bananas. I have no doubt that these yams are very nourishing, but I, for one, am heartily sick of them.'

'I think that would be a very good plan,' said Gub-Gub.

The next day about ten o'clock in the morning they passed the mouth of a beautiful river.

'That looks like a good place to get bananas,' said the Doctor. 'I think we'll steer the boat in there and see.'

So the ship's nose was turned towards the land, and presently they entered the mouth of a very lovely, wide stream. Passing up the river a few miles, between thickly wooded banks, they finally brought the ship to anchor close to a large town of straw huts.

This town happened to be the chief town of the Goo-Goo people – that is, the Gambia Goo-Goos – whose country stretched for some miles inland from this point.

The Doctor remarked at once that it was a much pleasanter country than the one they had left, and the town bigger and better built than that of the Jolliginki.

The swallows which were flying along over the Doctor's ship turned also when they saw the boat change its course, and, entering the river, they settled down upon the banks around the ship, causing great astonishment to the Goo-Goo people. The townsfolk were not accustomed to have many boats visit their harbour, but to have one come accompanied by a great flock of birds was, of course, something they had never seen before.

Stepping ashore, the Doctor was greeted by the Chief of the Goo-Goos, who asked him very politely if there was anything he could do for him. The Doctor made the Chief a present of an extra pocket-knife he had, and then explained that he needed provisions for his ship and that he had come into this port expecting to find at least some fruit.

The Chief of the Goo-Goos asked him what foodstuffs, besides fruit, he would like. And Gub-Gub smacked his lips while the Doctor reeled off a long list of eatables.

'I am not sure,' said the Chief, 'that I shall be able to get you all these, but I will get you as many as I can.'

He then gave orders to several servants and messengers who stood about him in attendance. And before long the Doctor and his animals saw a long line of porters going down to the ship with loads of food upon their heads.

'How wonderfully simple!' said the Doctor, watching them. 'Now, if I had stopped at Liverpool to have the ship provisioned it would have taken me a week to get that done.'

2

THE DOCTOR'S PLAN

JOHN DOLITTLE then thanked the Chief many times and asked him if there was anything he could do for him in return. But the Chief, who seemed no end pleased with his new pocket-knife, told him that no return or thanks were necessary – it was a pleasure, he said, and he hoped the Doctor would call again.

Returning to the river bank, John Dolittle saw that some great commotion was going on among the swallows. They had been joined by a number of green-breasted birds with whom they were now chattering and jabbering away in a very excited and agitated manner.

Now, it happened that this town of the Goo-Goos had been visited some months before by a white lady. She wrote books; she had short hair; she wore a collar and tie. She was, in fact, the kind of lady that was called in England in those days the New Woman. As soon as she set foot in Goo-Goo Land she had started bossing the Chief around, telling him how to run his country, how to bring up his children and a whole lot of other things which she thought he ought to know.

The chief had not liked her very much and was heartily glad to see her go home again. But the Goo-Goo wives had admired the New Woman tremendously. They had never seen husbands and chiefs bossed about before by women, having been all their own lives very obedient to their menfolk – as is the custom in Africa. They could not understand how the white woman worked this 'charm' – for magic of some kind, they thought, was the only thing that could give a woman such powers.

At last they decided that it must be in the strange hat she wore upon her head. This was a man's felt hat with a bird's wing on it – the wing of a green-breasted martin. So wanting to be like the New Woman who bossed men around, all the Goo-Goo wives had to have a felt hat with a martin's wing on it. With that, they thought, they would surely be able to boss their husbands as much as they liked.

This New Woman idea spread all over the Goo-Goo country. And although the Chief, terrified at the thought of having thousands of women in his land like the English writer of books, gave orders that it should stop, the New Women still met and worked in secret. And the poor martins were trapped and shot in great quantities to provide wings for felt hats.

Now, the martins – this particular kind was the green-breasted martin – are first cousins to the swallows. And they were now telling their troubles to those swallows who were travelling with the Doctor. This was what all the commotion was about which John Dolittle saw as he came back to his ship in the river.

When the Doctor got close to his ship six of the swallows who were leaders came to him and complained of the treatment that their cousins, the green-breasted martins, had suffered from the Goo-Goo bird hunters.

'If something isn't done about this soon,' said the swallows, 'the martins in this country will be wiped right out. It's a perfect shame.'

'But couldn't they go somewhere else?' asked the Doctor, 'to some other land where they wouldn't be hunted for hats?'

'At any other time they could,' said the swallows. 'But this is the nesting season for them. And the eggs and young birds cannot be left to get cold.'

'Humph! What do these martins live on?' asked the Doctor.

'Flies – the same as we do,' said the swallows. 'Mosquitoes and small moths are their favourite food. But they will eat any kind of flying insects. Now, in this country many of the mother birds whose husbands have been killed are dying of cramps, sitting on the nests afraid to leave to get food, and with no mates to bring it to them.'

'Dear me! This is a terrible thing,' said the Doctor. 'Terrible! I'll go back and speak to the Chief about it.'

So the Doctor went and asked the Chief of the Goo-Goos if he could not do something to stop the killing of these beautiful birds.

The Chief said he would do what he could and at once sent messengers throughout the whole of the Goo-Goo country with orders that the killing of martins must stop.

Then John Dolittle came back to his ship and sent word to the martins of what he had done. The martins thanked him, but asked that he remain here a few days to see if the orders were carried out.

So for some days the Doctor's ship stayed in the river, after it had been moved a little further from the town to a better anchorage. And John Dolittle now had time to travel up the stream by canoe to explore and see the country.

When he got back the martins came to him again, saying that the Chief's orders were not being obeyed, that two hundred more birds had been killed secretly and put on felt hats since he left.

For a moment the Doctor was silent, frowning with furious indignation. Then he asked that all the leaders of both the martins and the swallows meet him in the cabin of his ship right away to discuss the situation.

'Now, tell me,' said John Dolittle as soon as they had all found comfortable places around the big table to perch on, 'you martins live on flies, mosquitoes and moths, do you not?'

'Yes,' said the martins, 'but only on the smaller moths; the big fuzzy ones give the young birds hiccups. We like mosquitoes best – for summer diet there's nothing like a good, juicy mosquito.'

'Fine!' said the Doctor. 'Now, my idea is this: Mosquitoes sting people, you know – most uncomfortable. And moths eat clothes. And a lot of other insects, like flying ants and beetles, would be a fearful nuisance to people, if you birds did not keep them down by eating them. What I propose is that you should stop eating flies and insects for a while. They will then become a great pest. Then perhaps I'll be able to persuade the Goo-Goo wives to obey the Chief's orders and leave you alone.'

'But what are we to live on in the meantime?' asked the martins. 'We're not like finches and starlings; you know we must have insect food.'

'Ah!' said the Doctor. 'I hadn't thought of that.'

Then Gub-Gub, who with the other animals was listening intently (since the conversation was about food), said:

'Doctor, I have an idea.'

'Splendid!' said John Dolittle. 'What is it, Gub-Gub?'

'Downstairs in the hold of this ship,' said the pig, 'there are fifty packing-cases full of dried locusts. Why can't the martins live on them while you are bringing the Goo-Goo wives to their senses?'

'Excellent!' cried the Doctor. 'Do you think,' he asked, turning to the martins, 'that you could feed your babies on dried locusts for a while?'

'Oh, certainly,' said the martins – 'if we had to.'

'All right,' said the Doctor. 'Now, listen: We must make

a thorough job of this. I want you leaders to send out messengers to all the fly-catchers and insect-eaters in this district – martins, swallows, swifts, whippoorwills, shrikes, every kind. Tell them that dried locusts in plenty will be set out on the deck of this ship for them to come and eat and take to their young ones. But no live insect must be touched from now on till I give the word. Understand? And if we can't persuade the Goo-Goo ladies to change the style in hats within a very short space of time I shall be greatly surprised. The conference is over. Now, send out your messengers and keep me informed of how things are going.'

By nightfall the leaders returned to the Doctor and told him that his orders had been carried out. All the insect-eating birds (of which there are a great number of different kinds in Africa, a fine hunting ground for bugs) had willingly agreed to help by leaving all moths, mosquitoes and ants strictly alone.

3

SPEEDY-THE-SKIMMER

AND for the next two weeks the scene around the Doctor's boat was very gay, with myriads of brightly coloured fly-catchers of all kinds coming and going to feed on the dried locusts set out for them on the deck.

At the end of twenty days the results of the Doctor's plan were quite surprising – even to John Dolittle himself. For, you see, all the insects, now being left strictly alone by the birds, began to lay thousands and thousands of eggs and to have huge big families, and to multiply and increase in the most alarming way.

The first sign of success that came to those on the ship

was when Gub-Gub woke up in the middle of the night, crying out that he was all over mosquito bites. One by one the rest of the ship's company were awakened and kept awake by the stinging flies.

'Ah, hah!' said the Doctor, sitting up in bed and busily swatting in all directions. 'This is splendid. I wonder how the Goo-Goo ladies like this.'

But the mosquito plague grew and grew – more terrible every hour. Those on the ship really suffered a great deal for the sake of their friends, the martins. When the Doctor and the animals ventured on deck in the morning they found the air outside thick with mosquitoes and flying ants, and they were finally driven back by the pests into their cabin again. Then they slammed the doors shut and stuffed up every crack to keep out the swarming insects.

Poor Gub-Gub was a dreadful sight – he was, in fact, nothing but one large pink mosquito bite. The Doctor had to put him to soak in a bathtub of boracic acid to reduce the swelling. And as for the pushmi-pullyu, having no tail to use as a fly swat, he had a perfectly terrible time. But he never grumbled.

Of course, they could not very well stay shut up in the cabin without any fresh air for days on end, and soon the Doctor realized that he must get some protection from the flies for himself and his animals. So he sent for one of the swallow leaders.

In answer to his summons it was the chief of the leaders that came, a very neat, trim little bird, with long, long wings and sharp, snappy eyes. Speedy-the-Skimmer he was called, a name truly famous throughout the whole of the feather world. He was the champion fly-catcher of Africa, Europe and America. For years every summer he had won all the flying races, having broken his own record only last year by crossing the Atlantic in eleven and a half hours at a speed of more than two hundred miles an hour.

HUGH LOFTING

'Speedy,' said the Doctor, 'I and my party are imprisoned in our ship here. We dare not go out to take the air or stretch our legs for fear of the mosquitoes and biting flies. Can you do anything for us?'

'Why, certainly,' said Speedy. 'I'll tell off a few hundred wrens to mount guard over the ship here and keep the mosquitoes away from you and your party. They'll take care of you. Your scheme is working splendidly, Doctor. The Goo-Goo ladies are having a frightful time. They're much worse off than you are, you know, because they wear fewer clothes and the flies have more room to bite. I'll send you the wrens right away.'

So saying, Speedy flew off. And from that time on the Doctor's ship had a special guard of nine hundred wrens – very small birds, but marvellous fly-catchers. John Dolittle and his pets were now able to come safely out on deck and take the air and enjoy themselves.

Two days after that, in the morning before it was quite daylight, the Doctor said to Jip:

'I think I ought to go ashore into the town to see what's going on. I notice that the ants and beetles have started increasing at a great pace the last day or so. I am a little bit uneasy. I mustn't let this thing go too far.'

From the deck the animals watched the Doctor depart. For protection he had gloves on his hands, and his head, all but the eyes, was covered with a red handkerchief.

'I'm glad he didn't take any of us with him,' said Gub-Gub, who was now entirely recovered from his bites. 'Just look at the flies swarming around his head!'

It was not long after John Dolittle left that Too-Too, the owl, suddenly cried:

'Oh, look! Here comes the Doctor back, running. Goodness, he's all excited – waving his arms! See! I wonder what has happened in the town.'

Dab-Dab, Gub-Gub, Jip, Too-Too, the pushmi-pullyu and the white mouse crowded to the rail of the ship as the Doctor came bounding down to the river.

'What is it, Doctor,' called the owl as soon as the Doctor was within earshot – 'flies?'

'No,' gasped the Doctor, as he came panting up on the deck. 'Ants! – flying ants, black ants, red ants, white ants – ants in hundreds and thousands and millions. You can't see the houses any more – nothing but mounds and mounds of ants.'

'What has happened to the people?' asked Dab-Dab.

'They've shut themselves inside the houses. But the ants are eating the houses up – they're only made of grass. It's what they'll do when they've eaten the houses that I'm afraid of. Heaven help the people if the ants are still hungry then! Too-Too, get the Skimmer for me as quick as you can. Hurry, or the whole of Goo-Goo Land will be wiped out!'

4

THE MARTINS ARE SAVED

So off went Too-Too to find Speedy.

'My gracious! I had no idea matters had gone so far as this,' said the Doctor, sitting down and mopping his brow. 'It's lucky I went today to take a look at the town. I kind of thought that something was wrong. .... I do wish Too-Too would hurry. There isn't a moment to lose. Ah, good! Here he is – and the Skimmer, too.'

'Speedy,' said the Doctor as soon as the trim little bird had settled on the deck. 'The town of the Goo-Goos is being eaten up by ants. Tell all the fly-catchers to go back to work. Take them up yourself to the town and clear those ants away. Hurry, for pity's sake! It's the biggest job you ever had to do. You'll need every fly-catcher you can raise. And hurry, Speedy, as fast as you know how.'

Then the swift and famous Skimmer rose high in the air on his curved and flashing wings of blue. And reaching to terrific height, he began letting out shriek after shriek – a high, piercing whistling cry. Those on the deck of the ship below watched him as he swept the sky in dizzy circles, calling, calling, calling: 'Tee-wee-hee! Tee-wee-hee! Tee-wee-HEE!'

And very soon, in answer to the swallow leader's cry, fly-catchers of every description, colour and kind left whatever they were doing and came swirling into the air in a dark and ever-growing mass above the Doctor's ship.

Then suddenly, led by Speedy-the-Skimmer, the enormous army of birds made off for the town at a terrific pace. The rush of those millions of wings through the air was like the North Wind gone mad.

'Come along,' said the Doctor. 'We must see that the Goo-Goos are rescued from their plight. I started this – I've got to see it through.'

The animals all jumped up and followed him as he left the ship and raced off towards the town.

As they drew near to it a curious buzzing noise reached their ears. Tremendous – like some great machine purring, whirring smoothly – it grew and grew; the noise of millions and millions of insects working busily in the sun.

When the animals got closer the sight that met their eyes was indeed a strange one. You couldn't see the houses of the town at all. Over everything in view lay a thick moving carpet of ants.

'Golly!' said Too-Too. 'I'm glad I'm not a Goo-Goo. How on earth are they ever going to get out from under that mess?'

But even while he spoke the fly-catchers swept down upon the moving carpet in countless numbers. And then began the most terrific battle ever seen by mortal eyes.

It lasted three hours. And, although the fly-catchers won, by the time the last of the ants and beetles and moths and mosquitoes had been driven away, the birds were so exhausted that they sat and lay and squatted in panting, weary millions on the ground, hardly able to move their wings another flip.

And now could be seen what work of havoc the insects had done. The straw thatching of the huts was all eaten away; only the bare poles remaining. The shade trees before the doors were stripped of their leaves, bare, as though winter had come in a night. And from within the frames of the dwellings frightened, huddled families of black folk

gazed out at the white man and the millions of birds who
had saved them from destruction. Not a rag of clothing
remained among the lot of them, for the moths had eaten
every scrap of wool and cotton they possessed; not a ves-
tige of a roof remained above their heads and they themselves were covered with mosquito bites. But their lives
were saved. The Doctor and Speedy-the-Skimmer had
arrived only just in time.

In a little while the Goo-Goos came timidly out of the
wrecks of their homes, and then John Dolittle made a
speech to them.

'People of Goo-Goo Land,' said he, 'you have today been

rescued from a great and terrible danger. And it was these little green birds you see about you here that saved you – the same birds that, in spite of your Chief's orders, you shot and trapped to make hats out of. They came to me on my arrival in your land and complained. And, seeing no other way would bring you to your senses, I told them to stop doing the useful work which they do for you all their lives. That work is the eating of flies and insects. I hoped when you should see what happens when that work is stopped that you would realize how foolish you have been in killing them. Do you realize it now?'

Then all the wives who had wanted to be New Women rose up and shouted:

'We do, we do!'

'I am glad of that,' said the Doctor. 'Do you promise that the Green-breasted Martin shall for all time be safe and unharmed in your land?'

'We do, we do!' shouted the Goo-Goos. 'The Green-breasted Martins who saved our lives this day shall be a sacred bird in Goo-Goo Land for ever! Woe to anyone who touches a feather of the Sacred Martin! May the Fifty-nine Curses of Hullagoozelum fall upon his head!'

Then the Chief, in a deep, bass voice, began reciting the Fifty-nine dread Curses of Hullagoozelum for the benefit of anyone who should henceforth molest a martin:

'May his hammock strings break in the dead of night, letting him fall into the deepest mud. May he, when he rests beneath the palm at noon, have hard and knobby coconuts descend upon his head. May he –'

'That will do, please,' the Doctor interrupted. 'You can recite the rest of the Fifty-nine after I'm gone. I see that many of your community have been severely bitten by the flies. If those of you who wish for medical treatment will come down to my ship your injuries will be attended to.'

Then the Doctor and his animals moved off towards the

river. And all the Goo-Goos followed him, murmuring to one another:

'Truly he must be a great man whom the very birds obey – greater by far than the white woman who was insolent to chiefs, a disturber of the peace and a fake magician, leading us astray.'

And now for many hours John Dolittle, M.D., was kept more than busy attending to fly-bitten Goo-Goos. His supply of witch hazel, bay rum, boracic acid, ammonia and bicarbonate of soda soon ran out. And he had to get herbs from the jungle and boil them down and make more lotions for his many patients.

It was halfway through the night before he was done, and he was very weary. But the Goo-Goos, after his treatment, were feeling fit as fiddles. The Doctor then set to helping them rebuild their homes. These, being of straw, were quickly repaired.

Then a feast was made ready by the Chief's wives in honour of the Doctor, and everybody sat down, and there was much laughter and merriment.

The next morning the Goo-Goos provisioned the Doctor's ship with proper foods for the balance of the journey. There was bacon and flour, prunes and cocoa for the Doctor, parsnips and cabbages for Gub-Gub, and plenty of tea and sugar for everyone. They even remembered to include some bones for Jip and seeds for Too-Too and the white mouse. When they finally brought aboard two bales of hay for the pushmi-pullyu the hold was full to the hatches.

'Good-bye, good-bye!' cried the Goo-Goos as the ship slowly moved away from the harbour. 'Safe journey home!'

THE STORY OF THE MAGGOT

I

EXPERIMENT NO. 179

DOCTOR DOLITTLE had many curious interests; among them a desire to discover how different small insects and worms got scattered about the earth.

During one of the periods when the Dolittle family was living quietly at Puddleby-on-the-Marsh, the Doctor and I, Tommy Stubbins, were preparing a pamphlet on the subject of bug travels. The means by which geographical distributions had come about had interested the Doctor for a long time and he was working day and night to complete a particular experiment which he had begun that week.

Gub-Gub, the Doctor's pet pig, and I were discussing some minor details when the Doctor walked into the room with a tray of maggots.

'Stubbins,' said he, 'I want to do some experimental work with these. If you will come with me we will begin with listening machine number seventeen.'

This was a sort of amplifying and warming machine which the Doctor had built to make the tiny sounds of bugs and worms loud enough for human ears.

'Ugh!' grunted Gub-Gub, glancing into the tray. 'What gooey, messy-looking things!'

Without further delay the Doctor and I proceeded to our apparatus sheds and set to work. We had quite good results. It seemed that several of the maggots – particularly one large and lively white one – had somehow got the drift of Gub-Gub's remark and were considerably offended by it.

'He had no right whatever to call us gooey and messy,'

said the maggot. 'Personally, to me pigs and people are much more gooey and messy than nice, clean, athletic maggots. And we would be glad if you would tell him so.'

'And you know, Stubbins,' said the Doctor after I had written this down into a notebook under the heading Experiment No. 179, 'I quite sympathize with their feelings in the matter. This idea of – er – revulsion and dislike on the part of one member of the animal kingdom for another is quite baseless and stupid. Myself, I've never felt that way towards any living thing. I won't say that I'd choose a maggot or a snail to make a warm personal friend of. But I certainly would not regard them as being unclean or less entitled to respect than myself. I will certainly speak to Gub-Gub.

'Now we want to get some information from these maggots about their geographical distribution. I would like to know roughly over what parts of the world their species is to be found. This big fellow seems quite lively and intelligent. Just raise the temperature another five degrees, will you, Stubbins? And turn on a trifle more humidity. Then we will question him.'

To begin with, we had some difficulty in making him understand the idea, geographical distributions. Finally, after we had made several attempts, he said:

'Oh, I know what you mean: journeys and voyages, eh?'

As a matter of fact, it wasn't precisely what we meant, but the Doctor thought it best to let him go on. He seemed anxious to talk and it was quite likely that we might get the information we wanted more easily by this means than by trying to get a too difficult scientific idea into his head.

'We are, as you probably know,' he began, 'nut maggots. We never live in or feed on anything but nuts. Moreover, the nuts have to be of a certain kind – or, rather, two or three kinds. I have heard that at former times our people also lived on other things. But this was long, long ago, and

we have got so used to nut life now that I doubt if any
member of our species could exist in any other surroundings. Birds were our greatest enemies, a certain kind of
woodpecker being our deadliest. But so long as we kept inside the nuts, of course, we were pretty safe. And as this
was most of the time, the journeys and voyages we made
were not very large or extensive. Sometimes we would be
dissatisfied with the nut we were living in and would move
out of it, walk along a branch of the tree and into another
one. And then, other times, perhaps too many maggots
would be occupying one nut and all the meat would be
getting eaten up, and we would have to make a change for

that reason. Sometimes, on those occasions, when there were, we'll say, four of us in residence there, we would draw lots to see which of us had to move out.

'And again, sometimes we made, for us, the much larger journey from one tree to another. This was done when the tree had something wrong with it and the nuts were not ripening well. And at all such times of moving we had to be most careful that we were not seen by our bird enemies because, of course, at our pace even such journeys took quite a long time.

'You have asked me,' said the maggot, 'to tell you something of our society and community life. Of course, I don't know exactly what kind of things you'd like to hear about. We live in colonies – almost always. Yet there isn't very much social life with us. It is nothing unusual for maggots living on the same tree not to make one another's acquaintance throughout their whole lives. And often enough even those living on the same limb would never meet. No, I can't say that we are a neighbourly lot. It is only those that actually live in the same nut that know one another well – and sometimes they feel that they know one another too well. A nut, after all, is pretty close quarters.

'But news does get around, even in maggot society. In one colony where I lived some time ago there was considerably more social life than in most. This was because the nut-trees were in a somewhat wild part of the country on an old tumbledown sort of ranch. The farmers very seldom bothered us, spraying and pruning the trees the way they do in most places. And for some reason or other the birds were scarce, too. So we could move around in the open, if we felt so inclined, a good deal more freely than we usually do.

'In this colony there was a quite extraordinary character. He was a very fast traveller, for one thing, holding all the records for speed. He could hop out of one nut, travel along

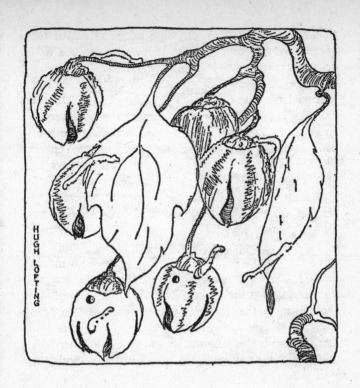

a limb and drill his way into another nut in quicker time than any of us. He was very daring, too. I've never known such an adventurous maggot. Even when he knew birds were around he'd hop in and out his front door, apparently just for the dare-devil fun of the thing.

'As it happened, he occupied at one time the same nut as I did myself – just the two of us. And I got to know him quite well. He was certainly an extraordinary individual. We often had long talks in the autumn evenings as we lay snugly curled up within the walls of our nut home and the wind without whistled and lashed the boughs of the tree around in the wildest manner.

'The autumn was liable to be a pretty troublesome time for us, because when the wind got really high the nuts that were getting ripe would often be blown to the ground.

'This happened to us one stormy night and I was glad I had my adventurous friend as a partner, I can assure you. Our home was blown clean off its stem and went bouncing down through the other branches and finally landed in the grass a good thirty yards away from the trunk of the tree.

' "Come along," said he, "we've got to get away from here – else the pigs will be around. They eat up all the windfalls – maggots and all."

'So, in spite of the wind and the cold, we crawled out of

our nut where it lay among the grass and set out on the long voyage of thirty yards to get back to the tree trunk.

'My gracious, what a journey it was, to be sure! You human animals, of course, cannot understand what difficulties, for a maggot, have to be overcome in a trip like that. You tramp through the meadows and underbrush as though they were nothing at all. But for us every blade of grass, every stick, every rootlet, every stone and leaf has to be climbed over laboriously.

'In the ordinary way, of course, when a catastrophe like that happened to a maggot home the rest of the colony would never expect to see the occupants again. One neighbour would say to another: "Did you hear about old So-and-So? His home was blown away last night." And, according to whether that particular member of the colony was popular or not, the other neighbour would reply: "Dear, dear! That's too bad." Or he'd just shrug his shoulders and say: "Well, it can't be helped." We took our neighbours' misfortunes – and our own, for that matter – philosophically. Indeed, I think I can say without boasting that we maggots are distinctly a philosophical race.'

2

DANGER AHEAD!

'S o you can easily see that when, four days later, my friend and I were sighted halfway up the tree trunk coming back to the colony and a new home, after being blown away in a full gale a distance of thirty yards, our reappearance caused no little commotion.

'Myself, I was too tired and worn out to move another step when we finally reached the top branches where the nuts were. But my adventurous and hardy friend at once set about hunting for a new nest to live in, one that should be in a good firm place where the wind wouldn't knock it down easily.

'In this he was assisted by other members of the colony. As I said, we are not a neighbourly lot as a rule, but the story of our sad catastrophe and plucky return had soon got around and there were many willing to help us.

'A big, sound nut in a good place was soon found and two strong maggots started to drill it for us. This, in our weary state, we were very glad to have them do, because late in the year, like that, the inner shell of the nuts is getting very hard and drilling is a slow and laborious business. We usually drill earlier, when the shell is softer.

'While our friends prepared a home for us, other maggots brought us food – which we needed desperately – and we rolled over on our backs and gave our feet a rest. When we were snug and safe inside we both curled ourselves up and slept like tops.

'It was late in the evening when we awoke. Both being terribly hungry again, we set to on the walls of our house and ate large quantities of nut. We found that we had chosen well, for our new home was juicy, sweet and ripe. To a maggot there is a tremendous lot of difference among the nuts on a single tree.

'We started talking over our adventures, and I found my friend was very dissatisfied that he had been born a maggot. He had a great and burning ambition to travel. In making him a maggot instead of a bird or a deer, Fate could not have been more unkind.

' "Just the same," said he, "I have no intention of letting it make any difference to me, so far as I can. I mean to travel. I enjoyed that wild journey the other night. It was a challenge. And though I was desperately worn out, it gave me the thrill of conquest, exploration and achievement."

' "But how," I asked, "do you hope to perform big jour-

164

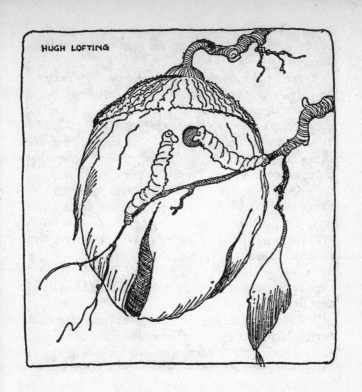

neys? It takes us days to move over a distance that the other creatures can do in a few seconds. It seems to me that for us it is much wiser to accept the life that was given to us and stay snug in our homes. We have no means of self-protection either. Almost any animal living can kill us if it wants to. Adventure is all very well, but I believe in safety."

'Before replying my friend raised his had, bit a piece of nut out of the wall and chewed on it through a moment of solemn contemplation.

' "Well, you know," said he at last, "I've been studying the other creatures a good deal of late. And I've come to the

conclusion that no matter what you're born – an elephant or a fly – life gives you certain handicaps. It is only by being adventurous that you can overcome those drawbacks and do what you want."

' "Humph!" I murmured. "I understand what you mean. Just the same, I can't see how a maggot is going to make himself into a great traveller."

' "Well," said he, "perhaps not a great traveller for a bird or a deer or a man. But I don't see why I shouldn't be a great traveller – for a maggot."

' "You're that already," I replied. "There isn't a member in the whole colony who doesn't admit that you've got more distance and speed – and nerve – to your credit than any of us. It seems to me that you're sort of hard to please."

' "Oh, pshaw!" said he, lying back luxuriously against the curved wall of our home and brushing his two seventh feet together to knock off some crumbs of nut. "I haven't done anything yet – nor been anywhere. Still, I may do – some day."

' "But I don't see how you're going to go about it," I repeated. "Our equipment for travelling is just ridiculous!"

' "There are other means of travelling," he answered, "besides one's own feet. Do you suppose that if Man – who is, perhaps, the greatest traveller of all – walked everywhere that he'd get –"

'At this moment our conversation was interrupted by someone scratching at the door. I arose and pulled out the husk material with which we always stopped up our holes to keep the wind out. To my surprise it was broad daylight. Having slept through the previous day, we had talked away the greater part of the night that followed. Outside, our neighbour, who lived in the next nut up the branch, was gazing in at me with alarm written all over his face.

' "Bad news, neighbour," he said. "The farmer is gathering the nuts. He and his helpers have begun at the lower end of the plantation. But they do not take long in stripping a tree. We are all getting out as fast as we can. I thought I would come and warn you, thinking you were asleep." '

3

THE MAGGOT GOES ON A JOURNEY

'WELL, you could have knocked me down with a feather. For many seasons, according to tradition anyway, the nut plantation had been neglected. The nuts had ripened on the trees, fallen to the ground in the autumn and either rotted or been eaten by pigs. No pruning or spraying had been done for years. And while we knew that this couldn't last for ever – because the trees were gradually spoiling for want of attention – still we never expected that a nut crop would be gathered from trees that had been so long left to themselves.

'I craned my neck out of our hole and looked backwards towards the south end of the plantation. And there, just as he had said, were men with ladders and poles and ground sheets stripping the trees of their fruit. In my tree, all about me, maggots were falling from the limbs above ours, hoping to drop into the soft grass and get away in time, rather than be gathered – with their homes – into the big baskets that the men carried. Panic had seized the whole colony. Of course, many struck the limbs as they dropped and were injured more or less; and still more, never aroused from their sleep, were gathered up with the harvest and taken away.

'I thanked the neighbour who had so kindly warned us, and he at once disappeared. Then I grabbed a large piece of nut that lay on the floor and called to my friend:

'"Come on! This looks like a voyage long enough to satisfy even you!"

'To my astonishment, he didn't even stir, just lolled back against the wall and smiled at me a reckless smile.

'"I'm in no hurry," he said quietly. "Who knows? The farmer's basket may be the very thing that will take me on a voyage worthy of my dreams. If they are harvesting this old, run-down plantation it must mean that nuts are precious this year. Why not stay and be – er – harvested, and, most likely, exported to foreign lands?"

'"But good heavens!" I cried. "You may be eaten, squashed – anything! This is madness."

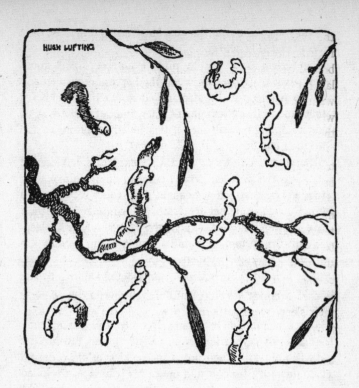

'Again he smiled, bit off another piece of nut out of the wall and chewed on it carelessly.

'"One has to be adventurous," he said, "if one would travel and see the world."

'Aghast, I gazed at him. What could one do with such a maggot?

'"You don't have to come with me," he said presently. "I admit it's risky. Do as you think best."

'Well, there had never been any question whatever in my mind about going with him.

'"I'm sorry," I said, "just the same, I wish you luck."

'And I stepped out of the hole and hurried down the tree-trunk as fast as I could go.

'I got clear only just in time. I suppose I was about twenty feet from the tree when the harvesters arrived and went to work on it. I had managed to reach a blackberry tangle, and in that I remained hidden and out of the way of their trampling feet till they had stripped the branches and filled their baskets.

'There were one or two little wizened nuts left on the tree. After the men had gone I climbed up again and took refuge in one that had got caught in a crotch between two limbs. It was quite secure from all winds and weather. There, almost a hermit, I spent the winter – mostly sleeping – till the spring sun came again to warm us into life and bring a new crop to the tree.'

'Very wise of you, indeed,' said Doctor Dolittle to the maggot. 'For, of course, it was impossible for your friend to survive.'

'That's where you're wrong, Doctor,' said the maggot. 'He *did* survive. My friend eventually returned, much older and wiser but still adventurous and reckless as of yore. And this is the story that he told me of his travels as we lolled once again in the security of a warm home while the night wind moaned through the branches:

' "After you had gone," my friend said to me, "our home was gathered into the big baskets, dumped into a wagon and taken away – with me inside it, of course. The wagon lumbered off out of the plantation and followed a hard, knobby road for quite a distance. Arriving at some kind of a warehouse the baskets were taken out and the nuts were dumped into big piles and stripped of their outer shells. I was a little afraid that my nut might be smashed in this business because it was done with heavy tools. And, watching from my open hole, I could see that many were spoiled and crushed in the process.

' "However, my home escaped injury and with thousands of others it was put into a packing-case, fastened up with nails and boards and set on one side to await some other kind of transport.

' " 'Well,' I thought, 'so far so good. I wonder where we go next.'

' "I did not have so long to wait. The next day we were again loaded into wagons and set off on still another journey by road. This was somewhat longer than the first had been, taking the best part of two whole days. At the end of it I realized with a thrill that we had come to the sea coast. So we were to go abroad after all! Our packing-cases were unloaded on to a wharf. My nut had fortunately been packed close to the outside of the case and right up against a crack between two of the boards. And so it was possible for me, when the case was standing right side up, to peep out from my hole and see what was going on.

' "There seemed to be great activity on the wharf. Numbers of men were running around, to and fro, loading stuff into a big ship. Such quantities of things! Sacks, bales, barrels, tin cans, kegs, boxes, everything. Our pile of cases was about the last thing to be put in. For this I was glad. I felt I'd stand a chance of seeing a little more of the voyage if I wasn't loaded down at the very bottom of the cargo.

' "But, as a matter of fact, it made no difference, because after we were slung up on the big derricks and dumped into the hold, heavy cover boards were put over us and fastened down with wedges, so we couldn't see anything anyway.

' "It was a long and tedious voyage and the inside of the ship smelled terribly. I didn't get seasick because, of course, any nut maggot gets so used to being swung about on the end of a tree limb that the motion of a ship is just child's play to him. But it was awfully monotonous.

' "One thing I was glad of and that was that after a week or so it began to get warmer all the time. This, I felt, must mean that we were coming to a pleasant country. I found a few other maggots in other nuts in my packing-case. And we helped one another pass the time away by chatting and guessing what the country would be like to which we were coming." '

4

THE SHIP'S RAT

' "No, I cannot say I cared much for the life of the sea as we maggots led it. Going visiting from nut to nut was about all there was to do. And before the voyage was over I knew the inside of nearly every nut there was in that packing-case. One advantage it had, however, and that was freedom from the dangers with which our life was usually beset. There were no woodpeckers or bug-hunting birds to bother us and no farmers to spray us with chemicals. Some of my fellow travellers said that they thought this was the ideal life and that no maggot could ask for anything better. But it hadn't nearly enough variety and excitement in it for me. By this time the nuts were getting dry and oily – the way people like them for the table – and we had all got so fat eating them that we could scarcely move.

' "Well, at last one day, after it had become quite hot, we heard a great commotion going on above us, the tramping of feet, whistle blowing, bell ringing and so forth. And soon the cover boards were lifted off the hold. We had arrived at some harbour. Our excitement was intense. I immediately hurried back to my old nut, the one near the crack in the packing-case, from which I would be able to observe things. Our case got slung up among the first loads. And while it was dangling from the end of the rope in mid-air I got a wonderful view.

' "Our ship was standing at anchor in the middle of a lovely wide bay. Smaller craft were moored up to us alongside to take off the freight. A couple of miles away across the blue water lay the most beautiful land I have ever seen. Purple mountains, clothed in palms and luscious jungle growth, rose against a cloudless sky. At the shore line a pretty little town, all white, clustered and shimmered in the sun.

' "And that was all I saw. Suddenly – I don't know exactly what happened – but some new strain was thrown on the rope that held us, dangling there between the sky and the deck. The seam or crack against which my nut was leaning gaped open a little wider. I don't suppose it was more than a quarter of an inch. But it was enough to let my nut out and it bounced upon the deck, nearly shaking me out of it bodily, then rolled away. My packing-case with all the other nuts – and the maggots, too – was lowered over the side to go ashore – without me!

' "Words cannot describe how I felt. After coming all that way to have this silly little accident upset my plans! And what was going to become of me now? My solitary nut was just sitting there on the open deck waiting for someone to step on it. A seaman kicked it out of the way with his boot. And I, with my house, was rolled into the scupper of the ship.

' "There a boy who was helping with the ropes picked it up and put it in his mouth to crack it. 'Well,' I thought, 'this is the end of my life of adventure.'

' "But fortunately it was a large nut with a good stout shell. While the boy was turning it around in his teeth trying to break it, one of the men bawled an order at him. He at once took it out of his mouth, put it in his pocket and went to work. If the man hadn't shouted the order at that exact moment I wouldn't be here to tell the tale. It was that that saved my life.

' "Presently, as the work at the ropes grew warmer, he took off his coat and laid it down on a windlass. There it remained for several hours till he finally took it up again and carried it down to his cabin. Here he hung it on a peg and did not put it on again all day. I was afraid, of course,

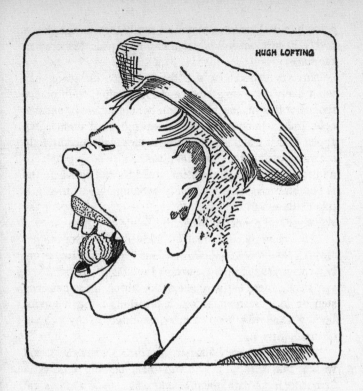

from moment to moment that he would put his hand in the pocket and, discovering the nut, complete the work of cracking and eating it.

'"But finally he came back to the cabin and went to bed. And after I heard him snoring sound asleep I sighed a great sigh of relief. I knew I was safe for the night anyhow.

'"Well, there I was, for the present out of danger it was true, but with no way of telling how long my security would last. Not beyond the morning, I felt pretty certain; and then I remembered that sailors worked in shifts or watches and that I could not be sure that the boy would sleep more than four hours.

' "I wondered if I had better get out of the nut right away and leave his pocket while it was still possible. My chances of reaching another nut in which to hide were not, of course, very good. For one thing, the packing-cases had most likely all gone ashore; and for another, the distance from the boy's cabin to the hold would be very considerable. There were other things I might hide in at a pinch, like apples and biscuits – even though they were not, strictly speaking, the kind of home that was proper or agreeable for a nut maggot. But the problem would be finding where the apples and biscuits were kept aboard ship – and then getting there myself.

' "I lay and pondered for quite a while over this – for me a very serious matter. Finally I decided to go. Even to get clear of the coat would take me, I calculated, going at my best speed, at least three-quarters of an hour.

' "When I was halfway out of my hole I heard a strange sound and drew back. It was a breathing noise, a sort of sniffing – and quite close. Within the safety of my nutshell I waited, listening.

' "It didn't take me long to determine what the sound was. It was a rat. I had heard them before. Nuts are a favourite food with them – and this one – a ship's rat – had smelt mine in the coat pocket and was coming after it.

' "I wasn't terribly scared, as a matter of fact, because I knew that my kind of nut had a shell that would take a rat a day at least to gnaw into. Still, I was annoyed because it certainly meant that my plans would be upset and delayed. Snuffling and panting, the rat climbed into the pocket. He found the nut right away, of course – and at once made attempts to gnaw it open. Realizing that it was a big job to get at its meat inside, he then took a grip of it by one end and started to carry it away.

' " 'Good!' I thought to myself. 'He will probably live

near the ship's foodstuffs. This may be a splendid way to get out of here. I'll sit tight and see what happens.' " '

5

TRIP TO THE GALLEY

' "And so, carried in the rat's mouth, I and my home left the pocket of the ship's boy's jacket and covered in ten minutes a distance which it would have taken me on my own feet weeks to perform. It was amusing to me to see how the rat handled the nut. It was heavy for him and, after he had carried it in his mouth for a few yards, he would set it down and roll it forward with his paws. Along beams, girders, through scupper holes, the stress of the work changing always with the roll and pitch of the ship, that rat somehow got my nut transferred from the quarters where the crew slept to the next compartment. This was a sort of storage room for sails and ropes. Here he evidently felt that he was safer than he had been in the men's cabin, because he left me and my nut a moment and went to fetch his wife. She, a large lady rat, came and inspected the situation with her husband. They conferred a long time. The nut was now on top of a big pile of canvas and the difficult job was before them of rolling it, or lifting it, over an enormous crease in one of the sails.

' "Suddenly their discussion was interrupted. The door of the sail room opened and two men in a great hurry entered to take away some sails. As the rats scuttled to safety my nut was rolled down off the pile. One of the seamen saw it go. He picked it up. And then, back I went into a pocket.

' " 'Dear me!' I thought. 'I am as badly off as before.'

' "The seaman went up on deck, carrying the sail with his

companion. There I found that we were now well out to sea
again and that darkness had come on. Wind and rain were
lashing across the deck. The men had hard work getting
the sail into place. I was carried in the man's pocket
high up into the rigging while he tied ropes and fixed the
canvas.

'"When he came down he was all wet with rain. Even
where I was, snug inside my nutshell, while the water did
not actually reach me, I could feel the dampness of his coat
and the wet atmosphere of his pocket. I was chilled to the
marrow."

'My friend never quite recovered from that chilling,' said

the maggot from inside the listening machine. 'We maggots are very sensitive to dampness – especially cold dampness. Rheumatism, you know, Doctor.'

'How extraordinary!' said the Doctor. 'I would have thought rheumatism was foreign to maggots.'

'Not at all,' replied the maggot. 'Our legs get quite stiff with it at times.'

The Doctor turned to me. 'Be sure and get that all down, Stubbins. It may prove very valuable in my experiments.'

The maggot waited a moment for me to finish scribbling and went on: 'My friend told me those few hours in that wet pocket stiffened him so he could barely walk for days. He was relieved when the sailor took off his coat and proceeded to shake the rain off it. For again Fate took a freakish hand in his affairs.

' "My nut was shaken clean out of his pocket," he said, "and went bounding across the floor into a corner."

' " 'What was that I dropped?' said the man as my nut clattered away across the room.

' "He got down on his hands and knees and began groping about the floor. Then he struck a match. I trembled for my safety. If he found it he would certainly crack the nut open – either with his teeth or his boot. Finally he spied it away off under a bunk in a far corner. For a while he fished for it with a stick. And then, to my great relief:

' " 'Oh, pshaw!' he said. 'It's not worth bothering with – just a nut.' And he went to bed.

' "And now, when I put my head out of the hole and looked about me, I found that I had been brought back to the same room where I was before. I imagine it was a sort of general sleeping quarters for all the sailors. They seemed to take it in turns to come down and have a rest there.

' "Once more I began to consider leaving my nut home and trying to reach the place where the foodstuffs were stored. But this time I hadn't more than a few minutes for

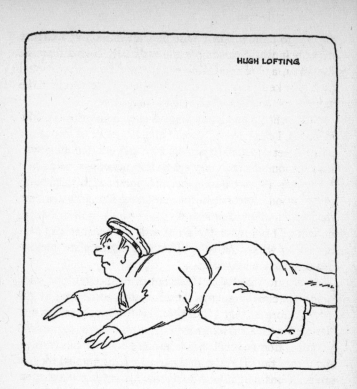

consideration before I heard the rat again. Getting my nut
out of the corner may have been difficult for the sailor, but
it was an easy matter for the rat. He gave one grunt as he
realized he had found his lost property, then promptly
picked it up in his mouth again and started off.

'"Neither was the sail room such a difficult territory for
him this time, now that some of the canvas had been re-
moved. With his wife's assistance he easily rolled my home
over to the far side, where they took it down a hole and
pushed it out into a third room.

'"This I knew at once, from the smells around, was a sort
of food store, eating place or kitchen. I decided now that I

had got to part company with my nut as soon as a chance offered. It was certain that the rat's home would not be far away, and if they once got the nut there they would probably keep gnawing at it until they got through the shell.

'"So, when their backs were turned a moment in consultation, I crept out of the nut and got away as fast as my chilled feet would carry me. They did not see me leave. And a moment later they rolled the nut down into their own hole and I never again set eyes on my home in which I had travelled so far and had so many hairbreadth escapes.

'"Well, I suppose that was about the riskiest thing I ever did in my whole life, when I crept out of that nut aboard ship, not knowing where my next shelter, nor my next meal, was to come from. The room was, as I had thought, a sort of kitchen. I guessed that it would not be used by the cooks before daylight. That should give me at least three or four hours to look around in. In a ship's kitchen anyway, it was a comfort to realize, I had no enemies but cooks.

'"From the floor I started out to find some table leg or other means of climbing upwards. I knew that foodstuffs would most likely be up high, on shelves in cupboards and the like. Finally, after a tremendous amount of work, I got to the upper levels. The shelves contained nothing but jugs, bottles, cups and dishes, especially arranged so that they could not fall from the rolling of the ship. I decided the food must be in the cupboards on the other side of the kitchen.

'"So there was nothing for it but to make the long, tedious journey down again to the floor, across and up the other side. I did it, though I was badly out of breath before it was over. Next came the job of getting into the cupboards. They were all locked. I hoped there might be space enough under the door to admit my small bulk. But there

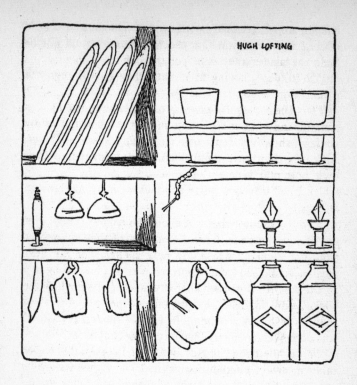

again I was disappointed. At length I hit upon the rather
ingenious idea of getting through the keyhole.

' "Inside I met with more bad luck. There were plenty of
foodstuffs there, but they were all in tins, tins with the
covers on. Getting into them was absolutely hopeless. I
turned away, retraced my steps through the keyhole and
began a general search around the kitchen. Perhaps I might
find some odd pieces of biscuit or apple lying around which
would serve as temporary shelter and food, till I could
establish more permanent quarters. But pretty soon I
realized that that too was out of the question. And the
reason was not far to seek. Any scraps or leavings were

taken care of by those wretched rats. There seemed to be dozens of them. Several I saw actually nibbling up crumbs from the table and the floor.

' "Well, you'd never guess where I finally took refuge; in a rat-trap! This contained a very old piece of ship's biscuit as bait. The rats knew it was a trap and they wouldn't go near it. And so I realized, as I crawled into it and noted the daylight showing through the porthole, that after all I was safer here than I might have been in any more regular food, from both rats and men." '

6

GARBAGE-CAN CANOE

' "WELL, it was a strange place indeed to travel in, the bait in a rat-trap. And yet I did it. I made that whole sea voyage, back to the port I had started from, in that mouldy piece of ship's biscuit, which – luckily – even the rats wouldn't eat. We went to many other ports before we got home. At some of these I was tempted to try getting ashore. But as I noticed we never stayed more than a day or so I decided that discretion was the better part of valour and I'd better stay where I was. My chances of finding a means of getting ashore in that short time were very poor.

' "And, I suppose, when all is said and done, things could not have turned out better for me than they did. My rat-trap was the safest place for a maggot on the whole ship. Our visits to all these other foreign ports served moreover to take up considerable time, so that by the date the vessel had got home again the winter was passed and spring had made outside travel possible for me once more. If I had arrived in the winter I could never have been able to go ashore without dying of the cold.

' "The problem of getting ashore bothered me a good deal. I worked out several plans while we were on our way back. But none of them seemed very hopeful. At length I determined to wait and see what chances offered themselves when I got to port. It was almost impossible to foretell what conditions I would be confronted with, anyhow. Which again, more by good luck than good management, proved itself to be the wisest thing I could have done. It is funny how throughout my whole voyage things seemed to be done for me, rather than by me, and always for the best.

' "After we moored up at our home port a good deal of cleaning was done about the ship. Among other places the kitchen was turned out and thoroughly scrubbed. The cook's assistant came upon the rat-trap and decided that since it hadn't caught any rats on a whole voyage it ought to have something done to it. He changed the bait, replacing my piece of mouldy biscuit with a hunk of yellow cheese. The biscuit, which he threw on the floor for the time being, was later swept up with some other rubbish and dumped into a wooden box.

' " 'Now,' I thought to myself, 'comes the serious question : Where is he going to throw the rubbish? If he shoots it overboard into the water that will be the end of me.'

' "The cook's assistant lifted the box wearily and carried it up the companionway to the deck.

' " 'So,' I thought, 'soon now the question will be decided : Overboard or where?'

' "He carried it at once to the side of the ship and then threw the whole thing, box and rubbish and all, into the river.

' "In that short moment when I was on my way through the air towards the water I gave up all hope. To swim a little, to be eaten by a fish or be drowned, was all I could hope for in the circumstances. But my star of good luck still seemed to be following me. The box landed on the water

with a loud whack! right way up. Being made of wood and containing no heavy rubbish, it did not sink. It settled in the water down to about half its own depth, and then, like a listing, waterlogged boat, it began to drift down the river with the outgoing tide.

'"A dozen gulls at once swooped upon it to pick out the tit-bits they liked. Now, mark how curiously Fate protected me: If the scrap of biscuit in which I travelled had been at the very top of the rubbish, I'd have been gobbled up by the first gull that reached the box. On the other hand, if I had been too deep down, I would have been below the water line and drowned before I could have scrambled higher. A large sardine tin on top of my biscuit protected me from the fighting, squealing gulls above and the rest of the rubbish below me kept me up out of the water.

'"Meanwhile, my gallant garbage-can canoe sailed on down the stream. After a little, when the gulls decided they had got all they could out of my strange craft, they deserted it and went off in search of other fodder. The river was wide, as most are near their mouths – and the box at first floated out into midstream. This looked bad, because, if we reached the sea, heavy weather would soon sink us, of course. But presently, to my great joy, I saw that a small cross-current near a bend was swinging our course over towards the left bank. I had now crawled out of the biscuit fragment and was perched on the edge of the box at the top, like a mariner on the lookout. The left bank of the stream had trees on it at the next bend – trees that overhung the water. Would we touch the land there? If we did, I could soon scramble ashore and all would be well.

'"Dear me! No castaway seaman ever watched more anxiously for his approach to land than I did to see where the currents would carry my box of garbage. Darkness was coming on. To go out on the bosom of the ocean meant certain destruction. My heart sank as the current that was swinging me over towards the shoulder of the land covered with alders suddenly seemed to bend back towards the centre of the stream. The rest of the river was pretty straight, and ahead of me lay the darkening sea with all its threatening, gloomy expanse. My box, too, was sinking somewhat lower, but there still remained about six inches of its sides above the surface of the stream.

'"And then just when things looked worst a strong wind sprang up, blowing from the right bank. Once more Fate had interfered to keep me alive. Across the quite powerful course of the current the breeze blew my crazy craft towards the shoulder and the alders. We touched an over-

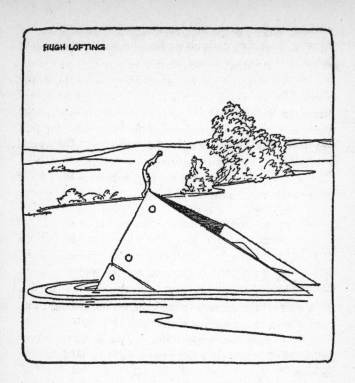

hanging bough that dropped into the water, and immediately we were brought to a standstill.

'"I wasted no time, you may be sure. Humping along as fast as I could go – for there was no telling how long we would remain moored in the stream which gurgled and swirled around the curves of the bank – I scrambled up on to a twig which touched the top of the box. Goodness! No words can describe my joy at feeling I was once more back on a tree. It wasn't a nut-tree of course, but to be on living wood of any kind after all those months of anxiety was something which nothing can convey to you unless you experience it.

' "Now alder trees, which are a swampy watery sort of thing, have a kind of catkins on them. They are not edible – for us maggots at all events – but I wasn't at all particular at the moment. I give you my word. There was a real storm blowing up of which the wind had been a kind of forerunner. In the half dark I found one of these berry things, which was partly dried, and drilled my way into it for all I was worth. The meat was bitter, but I was only looking for a shelter from the coming storm and a place to sleep. And once in, my goodness, how I did sleep! You couldn't have awakened me with a hammer." '

7

A RIDE ON A CANAL BARGE

'A MOST extraordinary story,' said the Doctor. 'I'm curious to know how he got back to you.'

'Well,' replied the maggot, 'I'm willing to go on if you are.' With that he gave a huge yawn and dug his fists into his eyes.

'Dear me!' cried the Doctor. 'You're tired. I must apologize for keeping you up so late. Tommy, that will be all for tonight. We can continue tomorrow, that is, if it's all right with the maggot.'

'Quite all right, Doctor,' said the maggot. 'But I would appreciate some food and a rest right now.'

John Dolittle then transferred the maggot from the listening machine to the tray where other maggots were busy eating bits of nut and apple.

'I hope the nuts I have supplied are the sort you care for,' he said to the maggot.

'Yes, thank you,' replied the tired worm. 'They are exceptionally good.'

HUGH LOFTING

'Well,' said the maggot the next morning after Doctor Dolittle had placed him in the listening machine. 'My friend's adventures were by no means ended. Of course once he was among real vegetation again life became almost a tame affair for him, even though he was not yet in his native country or anywhere near the kind of nut-tree which we always regard as home.

'But again a kind fate took him by the hand, as it were, and led him back to the very spot from which he had started. As he was making his way from one bush to another in a sort of general search for nut-trees along the river bank, he climbed into a flowering hawthorn. The voices of children reached his ears. And presently a party who had come a-maying stopped at the bush and began gathering the blossoming branches. Soon my friend found himself transferred from the bush to the arms of a small girl who was almost invisible behind the enormous bunches of bloom she was carrying.

'"I began by keeping very still," my friend told me. "Then presently when an opportunity came, while the little girl was looking the other way, I crept along the branch till I reached a dense tangle of leaves where I could hide myself. The branches had been tied at the bottoms into bunches with string. So I felt I would be safe here, at all events for a while. Being already very hungry, I ate a few of the hawthorn leaves and found them not half bad, though somewhat bitter in flavour.

'"And then I started out on still another stage of my journey, as part of the baggage of a picnic party. These children, with their aunt who accompanied them, lived, it seemed, in London. They had come out for a day in the country and were taking back the wild flowers to their city home. They went by coach – which probably made me the first maggot to travel by passenger stage. I saw something of the great city, too. Because when they arrived in London they left the coach and took a cab quite a distance through the thronged, busy streets before they reached their destination. Of course I could not see very much, not daring to creep out of the bunch of leaves too far. But I felt quite a thrill at travelling in this manner and listening to all the noises of the town.

'"At the children's home the bunch of hawthorn was placed in a big vase on a sideboard in the dining room. Here I lived as long as the flowers lasted, which was about a week. There was a dish of nuts on the sideboard, and at night I would creep down out of the flowers, drill my way into a nut, have a meal and creep back again.

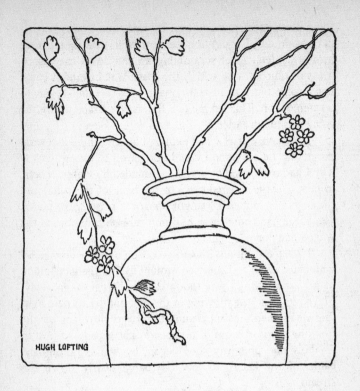

HUGH LOFTING

' "Later, when the flowers withered and were thrown out into the garbage can, I was once more faced with the proposition of foraging for myself. But while I was still wondering what I should do the man who emptied the garbage cans of that part of the town came along and carried me away. I was, of course, a little anxious as to where I was going to be taken.

' "It seemed a long distance. The wagon rumbled on and on until it got to the outskirts of the city. Then it stopped and the contents were dumped ino an empty plot near the edge of what seemed to be another river, but it turned out to be a canal. I wasted no time, but set off right away to get to some pleasanter surroundings. By this time it was getting dark again and I could not see very well, making my way mostly by feel. After scrambling up and down the assortment of objects with which the place was littered, I came upon some more solid thing made of wood and began to scramble up it. This led me to a flat, hard surface where the going was much easier.

' "It was only after I had explored around this for several hours that I discovered I could not get off it, except by the way I had come on. For it was surrounded by water. It was, in fact, a barge moored close to the bank of the canal and the object by which I had got aboard it was a gang-plank. The barge had come there to dump rubbish the same as the wagon had done.

' "I wasn't at all anxious to go off on another voyage by water just then, so I scurried around to find the gang-plank to get ashore. But I was too late. It had been taken away. The dawn was just showing in the east and by its pale light I now saw men moving around the barge, throwing off the mooring ropes. A team of horses was harnessed to a post in the bow and presently they began, by walking along the banks of the canal, to tow the barge slowly down the stream.

' "I was in despair. The barge contained nothing in the way of food or shelter and, as far as I could see, there was no getting off it. I sat there for about an hour watching those horses plod along, dragging the barge through the canal. Suddenly, the landscape began to look familiar. First a tree, then a piece of open field, and then I recognized *our* tree upon a ridge. It was the plantation where I had left you, my friend, so long ago!

' "But the barge wasn't stopping – it was going by! How to get ashore? I couldn't swim, yet the distance to the land was short – not more than six feet. The tow-rope, I realized, was the only connexion with dry land. For one wild

moment I had a notion to scale the bow-post and walk this two-hundred-foot tightrope to the horses' backs. But how to get down after I got that far stopped me. I'd never be able to jump from such a height. And as for crawling down the horse's leg – that was impossible.

'"So, desperately watching my native country slipping by at the rate of three miles an hour – a truly breakneck speed to a maggot's mind – I cudgelled my brain for some other means of getting ashore. I crept out over the counter and, standing on the vertical side of the barge, I saw that some of last year's leaves were floating on the surface of the stream. A wind had blown them off the banks. If I could only get on one, it might serve as a raft to reach the bank. Then, at great risk of being washed off by lapping wavelets, I crept lower still till I was less than a quarter of an inch from the surface of the water. There I waited for a leaf to float by near enough for me to step on to it.

'"At last one did brush past, touch the side of the barge right beneath my nose. I was only given a second to make the change. A misstep meant certain death. Yet I did it. With my rear legs still gripping the side of the barge I took hold of the leaf with my front pair. Then I let go! I flopped into the water with nothing but my nose out! But the leaf was a stout one. It didn't tip up while I slowly drew myself aboard it.

'"After the barge had gone on a few hundred yards or so, and the ripples of its wake had died away, I noticed to my horror that the leaf on which my life depended was simply surrounded with fishes. They were all watching me like tigers; their eyes shining as bright as coloured marbles through the water.

'"As yet there were only small fry around me. But very soon their interest began to attract the larger ones. Before a moment had passed the water around my leaf was full of big, evil-looking shadows, cruising silently around, waiting for a chance to snap. I kept myself curled up in the centre of the leaf – feeling somewhat safer there. But, although a favourable wind was carrying the leaf slowly towards the bank, there was no telling when the larger fish would grow bold enough to nip it down under the water and snatch me as I sank.

'"About three feet from the shore, realizing, I suppose, that their prey was escaping from them, they began. One big fellow made a leap out of the water bodily, curving over as he came down, evidently calculating on striking the centre of the leaf's top. But fortunately, the wind freshened just at the moment and he fell harmlessly

into the water with a splash, missing his mark by two inches.

'"After that they went for me hot and heavy. Fish after fish, some of them nearly a foot long, struck at the leaf – sometimes two or three together. But their wild competition came to my assistance. One large fish, pushed out of the way by a still larger one, snapped at the shore-end of the leaf – the second grabbed at the other end. And between the two of them they flicked the leaf bodily into the air off the surface of the water – rather the way you can, by bending it, snap a card out of your fingers and make it jump.

'"I had lost my hold by now and was catapulted up still

higher than the leaf. I must have been thrown a good four feet into the air! I could see the fishes watching me greedily as I sailed upwards. I shut my eyes, expecting to slip down the throat of one of those gaping monsters. When, plop! I landed, stunned, on the bank. I was safe in the soft grass!"'

The maggot, talking from the listening machine, stopped and looked off into space. I was writing furiously, trying to get everything down word for word.

'I do hope he wasn't injured,' said the Doctor.

'No,' replied the maggot, 'he was quite all right when he came out of his daze. You see, he was now only a few hundred yards from his home. It took him four weeks to cover those yards. And that is how he came back to me and to the home tree from which he started.'

'It's strange he didn't turn up when I gathered you and your friends for this experiment,' said John Dolittle.

'No, not strange,' said the maggot. 'He didn't stay more than a couple of months before he was off on another adventure.'

'You don't say,' replied the Doctor. 'I should have thought he'd had enough travelling.'

'Not my friend,' said the maggot. 'You know how it is, Doctor. Once a person starts wandering there is no keeping him at home.'

'Humph!' muttered John Dolittle, smiling. 'I know what you mean.'

THE LOST BOY

I

LONDON ZOO

DOCTOR DOLITTLE, Cheapside, the London sparrow, and Becky, the sparrow's wife, were in the Zoological Gardens looking for birds of all sorts to sing in the Doctor's Canary Opera. On the way to the bird enclosure they came upon many signs which read: *'Lost Children Will Be Taken To The Ladies' Cloak Room.'*

'Yes,' said Cheapside, noticing the Doctor reading this sign for the third time. 'That's so the mothers and fathers and uncles will know where to look for their nippers when they get lost. Folks is awful careless. On Saturdays and Sundays the Ladies' Cloak Room is just full of little lost Willies and Aggies. I always used to say they ought to learn 'em tricks and put 'em in a pen alongside the monkeys.'

Shortly after this, as the Doctor was passing one of the ponds for waterfowl, he noticed a small red-headed boy trying to wade out to feed the ducks. Fearing he might tumble in, the Doctor leaped over a low railing and grabbed the child by its pinafore. Then he looked around to find the youngster's mother or guardian. But no one at all seemed to be with him. The Doctor questioned him, but all the boy would answer was:

'I want to feed the ducks.'

'Take him to the Ladies' Cloak Room, Doctor,' said Cheapside. 'Don't argue with him. He's lost, all right. Come along. I'll show you the way.'

So, with the Doctor leading the little fellow by the hand, they set off along a winding path through shrubberies.

HUGH LOFTING

At the cloak room the woman in charge took the child and thanked the Doctor for bringing him.

'This is the second time he's been brought back today, sir,' said she. 'I've no idea who owns him. No one has put in a claim.'

'I don't wonder at that,' whispered Cheapside to Becky at the door. ''E's no beauty. I wouldn't be surprised if they lost 'im on purpose.'

'Sh!' said Becky. 'Maybe 'e's heir to a throne or something. I've heard tell how princes was lost deliberate by wicked uncles and things.'

'Heir to a kitchen chair!' snorted Cheapside with

disdain, ''E aint no prince. Princes don't 'ave 'air that colour.'

The boy seemed to have taken a liking to the Doctor. For when he was left in the woman's charge he bawled heartily at John Dolittle's departure. And about half an hour later, when the Doctor was busy conversing with the birds in the East Aviary, he suddenly found the red-headed child once more standing beside him.

''E's escaped from the cloak room again,' said Cheapside in disgust. 'Better tell the woman this time to lock 'im in the cupboard – or maybe we'll be arrested for kidnappin' before the day's over.'

Once more the Doctor returned the lost one to the care of the woman in charge of the cloak room. And this time he gave her special instructions to guard him carefully till his parents came for him.

'Dear me!' said John Dolittle, as he hurried back to the aviary. 'This has wasted quite a little of our time. I wonder who he is – look, it is beginning to get dark. We had better abandon our search for today.'

In spite of the lateness of the hour and the growing darkness, Mr and Mrs Cheapside insisted on seeing the Doctor home. And together they left the Zoological Gardens and set out for Greenheath.

'I'll probably decide on pelicans for the bassos and flamingoes for baritones,' said the Doctor. 'The higher voices we can do with linnets and such like, which we will get from the fields. Do you think you would be able to get me some pelicans and flamingoes, Cheapside?' the Doctor asked as they made their way through Regent's Park.

'Well, maybe,' said the sparrow. 'I know of one place about ten miles from the city where a rich feller has a whole lot of fancy waterfowl – pelicans among them. How many would you want?'

'About six, I should think,' said the Doctor, 'and six flamingoes, too. But eight or ten would make a better chorus.'

'Yes, that would be enough to sing anyone to sleep – for good – I should say,' murmured the sparrow. 'Maybe there's that many at this feller's place. I'll take a run over there in the morning and let you know. I ain't sure about the flamingoes. Maybe I'll have to go elsewhere for them. You wouldn't want to buy them, would you?'

'Not if the gentleman will lend them to me,' said the Doctor. 'You see, the – what's that white, shadowy thing over there, hopping about among the trees?'

'What – where do you mean, Doctor?' asked Cheapside, peering through the trunks of the dim-lit park.

'Funny! It's gone now,' said the Doctor. 'I could have sworn I saw something pop behind that elm over there, the other side of the beds. Perhaps it was my imagination.'

'Maybe some animal's got out from the menagerie – a deer or something,' said Becky. 'If it is, good luck to him, I say. I'd hate to live in captivity.'

'Yes,' said the Doctor. 'I dislike the idea myself of animals being confined against their will. In my private Zoo in Puddleby the cages all had locks on the *inside*, so the animals could get out when they wanted or shut themselves up at night just for the sake of privacy, you know. But, oddly enough, although they were all free to go when they chose, none of them ever ran away.'

'Yes,' said Cheapside, 'but yours was a real Zoo, Doc – run on proper lines. You always had a waiting list of animals to get *in*, instead of out. Goodness, don't I remember that old sleepy black bear you had who could never wake 'isself up in time for breakfast! You ought to 'ave seen that Zoo, Becky. Beat anything we saw on the Continent. Old Mr Bear asked the Doctor for an alarm clock. And every night when he locked his own door, to keep out the tramps and the rats, you'd 'ear 'im a-windin' that old tin time-piece of 'is. O' course, 'e couldn't tell the time – used to look at the back, instead of the face, pretendin' 'e knew 'ow. But 'e knew enough to get up in time for breakfast when it went off in the mornin'! Ah, that was a real Zoo, that was – bless me! What's that runnin' be'ind us? Didn't you 'ear footsteps?'

2

JOHN DOLITTLE BRINGS HOME A GUEST

THEY were now come to the edge of Greenheath. And the wide open common, dotted with gorse clumps, stretched before them in the dim starlight. The three of them paused, listening.

'Hark to me, Cheapside,' whispered Becky. 'I believe there's something following us. Let the Doctor go on ahead and you and I hang back and do a little scouting. I think I 'eard something moving the other side of those bushes over there.'

So the Doctor went on his way across the common of Greenheath while Mr and Mrs Cheapside hung back. And, keeping near the ground, where they would not be seen in the dim light, they set to work to find out who or what it was that was following them.

John Dolittle had pretty nearly made up his mind that it must be some animal, possibly escaped from the Zoo, that was determined to attach itself to his household. He had experienced this before many times. So great was his reputation among animals of every sort that he was constantly followed by lame dogs, rabbits, moles – all sorts of beasts who wished to consult him medically or see if they could be taken into his private circle of pets. But, the Doctor

argued with himself, if it was nothing more than that why did the creature not come forward to see him, instead of slinking around like this in concealment?

As he walked forwards over the springy turf of the heath John Dolittle expected the sparrows any minute to overtake him with news. But a good quarter of an hour passed without his hearing anything. And he could see the outline of his own circus tents not more than a few hundred yards away before Cheapside alighted on his shoulder and giggled:

'What d'yer think, Doctor? It's our red-headed friend, the nipper who was lost in the Zoo.'

'Good heavens!' cried John Dolittle, stopping short. 'The boy we left in the cloak room?'

'The very same, Doctor,' said Cheapside. 'If I was you I'd turn around and go back through the city some other way. That's about your only way of losing 'im.'

'But, my gracious, Cheapside, I can't do that!' said the Doctor. 'The child's lost. I can't leave him to wander around in the night like this. Where would he get supper? Where would he sleep?'

'Good lord, Doc!' said the sparrow impatiently. 'That ain't your concern. What are you goin' to do, adopt 'im?'

'Well, I certainly can't leave him out here,' said the Doctor. 'Where is he? I'll have a talk with him.'

So Cheapside guided the Doctor back a few yards to where Becky was keeping an eye on the boy behind a clump of gorse.

'Hulloa, my friend,' said John Dolittle in a kindly voice. 'Didn't your parents come for you at the Ladies' Cloak Room?'

'No,' said the boy.

'But how did you come to be lost at the Zoo?'

'I wasn't lost by my parents,' said the boy. 'It was I who lost my parents. I want to be a menagerie keeper. So I ran away from home and came to the Zoo. But they would keep taking me to the Ladies' Cloak Room and saying I was lost. Then when it began to get dark and I saw they were going to close up the place I thought I'd follow you.'

'Why?' asked the Doctor.

'Because I like you,' said the boy.

'But what of your mother and father?' asked the Doctor.

'Oh, they're all right,' said the boy. 'They've got lots more children. I set out to seek my fortune – I want to be a menagerie keeper.'

HUGH LOFTING

The Doctor took out his watch and peered at it in the dim light of the stars.

'Humph!' he muttered. 'There's nothing else for it. You had better come and spend the night with me. And to-morrow I must try to get in touch with your parents.'

'Who's that?' asked Gub-Gub as the Doctor entered his wagon leading the red-headed youngster by the hand.

'This is a young man who followed me all the way from the Zoo,' said the Doctor, as the animals all gathered about him examining the small stranger. 'He will spend the night with us. But I must get busy in the morning and find out who his parents are. Otherwise I may get arrested for kidnapping.'

'For catnipping, did you say?' asked Gub-Gub, the pig.

'No. For kidnapping,' the Doctor repeated – 'that is, for stealing him. Some people might not believe that he followed me so far. Have you got some extra sheets, Dab-Dab?'

'Oh, I suppose I can find him a shakedown somewhere,' said the housekeeper, wagging her tail in a harassed manner. 'Tut! tut! I wonder you wouldn't have more sense, John Dolittle, than bringing him here when you know the wagon is so crowded already.'

'But I didn't bring him,' said the Doctor. 'He followed me, I tell you I couldn't leave him out on the heath, with no blankets or anything.'

'Well, anybody else would have found some other way out of the difficulty,' snorted the duck. 'It's bad enough to have you bringing in stray animals of every kind. But children! You don't realize what you've let yourself in for. Children make a terrible mess of a home. Gub-Gub will have to give up his bed and sleep on the floor.'

'Oh, goodness!' groaned the pig. 'What with dieting for the opera and sleeping on the floor, I might as well be –'

At this point Matthew Mugg entered the wagon. In a few words the Doctor told him about the boy and the necessity of putting him up.

'Why don't you let him sleep in the menagerie, Doctor?' said Matthew. 'There's two or three empty stalls there, with lots of clean straw.'

'Did you say a menagerie?' asked the boy, his large round eyes showing intense interest. 'What is this place?'

'This is a circus,' said the Doctor – 'the Dolittle Circus. And I am John Dolittle, the manager.'

'A circus!' cried the youngster, stepping on Gub-Gub's tail in his excitement. 'But how splendid! I set out to seek my fortune and I've found it. It's just like Dick Whittington. I wanted to be a keeper in the Zoo. I thought you must be something interesting when I saw you talking to the birds, like St Francis. Of course I'll sleep in the menagerie. I'll sleep with the elephant.'

The boy, in spite of his being clearly tired from his long walk, was now all agog with the interest of his new position. He asked a thousand questions at once. And when supper was brought on he was so absorbed by the animals sitting around the table like people that he hardly ate anything. John Dolittle did his best to dissuade him from sleeping in the menagerie. But he was absolutely determined to spend the night with the elephant. And finally the Doctor had to carry him over there, almost too sleepy to keep his eyes open, and put him to bed under a pile of blankets. Alongside the enormous animal he looked like a grasshopper next to a horse.

'Now, for heaven's sake,' said the Doctor to the elephant, 'don't roll in your sleep. If necessary, stay awake. It will only be for one night. Tomorrow I hope to get this young man back to his parents.'

3

TROUBLE AT THE CIRCUS

AFTER spending a sleepless night himself, wondering whether the elephant had rolled on the child, the Doctor sped across to the menagerie almost before it was daylight. There he found the would-be keeper busily washing the elephant's face with a flannel. The enormous creature, realizing that the young tyrant meant well, was bearing the

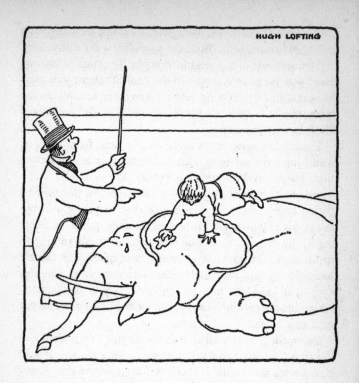

performance with patience while the boy walked about over his face, scrubbing it vigorously.

'I wish you'd take him away and let me get some rest,' said the elephant miserably in answer to the Doctor's 'Good morning.' 'I've hardly had a wink of sleep all night. I was so scared by what you said. When I did doze off I kept dreaming that I had squashed him out as flat as a pancake. And the first thing he did when he awoke – before I had a chance to get up – was to find a cake of soap and a floor rag and start cleaning my ears. I hardly slept a wink.'

'Neither did I,' said the Doctor.

The boy had now got hold of the menagerie broom and was busy brushing the elephant's hair with it.

'Er – pardon me,' said John Dolittle, taking it from him. 'But large animals don't have to have their hair brushed or their faces washed in the morning. They make their own toilet. How would it be if we went across to my wagon and had some breakfast?'

After a good deal of coaxing the young adventurer was taken off – much to the poor elephant's relief – to the manager's van.

The first thing that Gub-Gub said when they entered the wagon was:

'Doctor, I didn't sleep a wink all night. I shall have to go to bed immediately after breakfast.'

'Yes, and he kept me awake, too,' growled Jip, the dog – 'groaning and scratching the floor with his feet to make it soft!'

'Humph!' said the Doctor. 'But you were not the only ones who did not sleep. Well, let's have breakfast, then maybe we'll all feel better.'

'I told you you were in for something, Doctor,' said Dab-Dab as she set the porridge on the table. 'Children are a handful. One child is more nuisance than a dozen animals.'

'Yes, perhaps you're right, Dab-Dab,' said the Doctor, sitting down. 'I wonder why that is. Are you ever sorry you weren't born a man, Jip?'

'Good lord, no, Doctor!' said Jip. 'I wouldn't be a man for anything.'

'Why?' asked the Doctor, reaching for the cream.

'Men – people – worry such a lot,' said Jip. 'Their life is so – er – so complicated, difficult. Dogs never worry unless they're hungry or cold – or when they've lost their friends. Oh, no, I'm glad I wasn't born a man.'

'That's rather curious, you know,' said John Dolittle. 'There have been philosophers who say that people are born over again – that some men have been animals and some animals men. It's called the theory of reincarnation.'

'Then I bet Gub-Gub was a cook last time he was on earth,' said Jip.

'Well, you can be sure I was a good cook, then, anyhow,' said Gub-Gub indignantly. 'I'll bet you I never served up anything as poor as this diet gruel. I'll be glad when that opera's over! This training is ruining my disposition.'

The small red-haired adventurer apparently was highly pleased with his new home and had no intention of ever leaving it. All day long he insisted on helping with various parts of the show. He succeeded in getting in everybody's way to such an extent that it seemed that if something wasn't done about him soon there would be a general strike in the Dolittle Circus.

During the main performance in the big tent his determined efforts to take part in the show nearly cost him his life, when the lion stumbled during a balancing act and sat on him heavily. And the Doctor soon realized that Dab-Dab had been quite right and that one child could make more trouble than a dozen animals.

Seeing that it was urgently necessary to get him back to his home as soon as possible, the Doctor made a special trip into the city and put an advertisement in all the papers that a lost child with red hair could be claimed at his establishment on Greenheath. Meanwhile, the youngster, realizing the dream of his life, continued to have a wonderful time and to make himself what he thought was useful. He went into the clown's dressing room when no one was looking and daubed grease paint all over his face and pinafore. He called on the snakes during their performance and upset the tent and brought it down on top of the audience that was gathered there. He inspected the pushmi-pullyu, the two-headed animal, and made that poor, patient animal give him a ride on his back. He went to the performing

HUGH LOFTING

otters' tent and fell in their tank and nearly drowned before they fished him out.

By nightfall, when the Doctor and Matthew were reduced to a state of complete exhaustion, keeping him out of harm and mischief, the young adventurer announced that he intended to sleep with the elephant again tonight. And in spite of that poor animal's begging to be allowed to get a good night's rest undisturbed – and the Doctor's trying for half an hour to dissuade the boy from his intention – he finally went to bed with his big friend, much to the relief of everyone except the elephant.

'I don't know what I'll do,' said the Doctor to Dab-Dab

after supper, 'if his parents don't come for him tomorrow. Advertising in the paper is about the only hope we have. I had expected that they'd be here today.'

'It's your own fault,' said Dab-Dab, 'for bringing him here. You should have taken him to the police station.'

'That's an idea,' cried the Doctor. 'Why didn't I think of that? Oh, but he wouldn't like it. He is having an awfully good time here.'

'And what about the time we're having?' asked Dab-Dab. 'You'll have that poor elephant sick again if you don't get that little imp out of here – and you know what a handful he is when he's sick. I saw him just break down and weep when he heard that the child was going to sleep with him again tonight. Take the little nuisance to the police station. They'll be kind to him – and they'll find his parents a lot quicker than you can.'

'Humph!' murmured the Doctor. 'I suppose there's something in what you say. Well, if his parents don't come in the morning I'll take him over there.'

No one showed up the next day to claim the boy and Dab-Dab kept at the Doctor till she made him do as he had said he would. And about noon John Dolittle set out with the young man and left him in care of the local superintendent of police.

Everyone in the circus, especially the poor elephant, was greatly relieved to learn that he had gone, and the whole staff, which had been on the verge of open riot for two days, settled down once more to a peaceful life.

All that night again the Doctor hardly slept. This time his worry was not that the elephant might roll upon the boy, but how the youngster was getting on at the police station.

'You know, Dab-Dab,' he said at breakfast next morning, 'it seems such an inhospitable thing to do. The lad was having such a wonderful time here. And although I know, of course, that the police will treat him nicely, children are so funny, you understand. I couldn't help admiring the youngster – such pluck and determination – following me all that way from Regent's Park. And then for me to turn him over to the police! It's been bothering me all night. I think I'll run across as soon as I've had breakfast and see how he's getting on.'

'Oh, for heaven's sake!' said Dab-Dab wearily. 'I know what that means. Now, you listen to me, John Dolittle; that boy could get along and take care of himself anywhere. Don't you worry about him.'

'Yes, perhaps,' said the Doctor. 'But just the same – hulloa! What's this?'

At that moment two policemen in uniform appeared at the wagon door. Between them stood the red-headed boy.

'Heavens preserve us!' cried Dab-Dab. 'Here he is, back again. And you were going to go after him!'

'Good morning, sir,' said one of the policemen. 'The Superintendent presents 'is compliments and says would you mind taking this young man back into your charge? Every effort, the Superintendent says, will be made to find his parents. But in the meantime if you wouldn't object to keepin' 'im, the Superintendent will be much obliged.'

'Why,' asked the Doctor, 'wouldn't he stay with you?'

''E didn't seem to care for the station house, sir,' said the constable. ''Owled and 'ollered all night, saying 'e wanted to go back to the menagerie. And the Superintendent says – beggin' your pardon, sir – 'e reckons that's the proper place for 'im. 'E's broke all the windows and nobody got a wink of sleep – prisoners and neighbours and everyone complainin'. It seemed as though the only thing to pacify 'im was to fetch 'im back 'ere. So the Superintendent tells us to bring 'im and deliver 'im to you at all costs.'

The small boy, now that he was back in his beloved circus, was wreathed in smiles. He greeted all the animals in turn – who didn't seem nearly as pleased to see him as he was to see them. The Doctor rose from the table a moment to put the canary cage out of his reach. And when he turned back to the door again he found that the two policemen had sneaked off without waiting for further words and left the young adventurer on his hands once more.

4

THE GUEST DEPARTS

'WELL,' snorted Dab-Dab, 'perhaps in the future you'll believe me, Doctor.'

'Oh, yes, indeed, Dab-Dab. I agree that there's a lot in what you say,' said John Dolittle as the young man pulled the lamp down on the floor with a crash. 'Children are sometimes – er – a trial. But, you know, in some ways I'm sort of glad to see him back again – no, those geraniums don't need any more water, young man. I gave them some water before breakfast. Besides, that's hot water. You know, after all, Dab-Dab, this is a children's circus. It seems sort of proper that we should have one child on the staff.'

'If you do you won't have anybody else on it – long,' snapped the duck.

'Perhaps his parents don't mean to claim him at all,' said the Doctor thoughtfully.

'Heaven forbid!' said Dab-Dab devoutly.

'Maybe we can train him,' murmured the Doctor thoughtfully.

'Then train him to keep away from me,' said Dab-Dab, as the child upset the coffee-pot over the clean table-cloth.

HUGH LOFTING

Once more the Dolittle Circus was thrown into a state of turmoil by the return of the strange young person whose determination to be a menagerie keeper had already caused so much trouble.

One of the first things to happen that day was the appearance of the circus' regular menagerie keeper at the door of the manager's van.

'I've come to give notice, Doctor,' said he.

'Why, what's the matter?' asked John Dolittle.

'That young nipper's the matter,' said the man. 'I ain't 'ad no rest since 'e's been around. I warned you that I'd have to go unless he stayed away from my animals. Then

when I 'eard 'e'd been took off to the police station I supposed we were going to 'ave some peace. But this morning
'e's back again and 'is interference and tricks is worse than
ever. I want to give notice.'

'Well,' said the Doctor, 'of course, if you've made up
your mind, I wouldn't try to persuade you to stay. Have
you got another position in view?'

'I don't need no other position,' said the keeper. 'Since
you've been running the show on the sharing system I've
saved up a tidy penny. And now we're in London I'd like to
take a small shop somewhere and settle down.'

'Oh, then it isn't only on account of the boy that you

216

want to leave?' said the Doctor. 'Well, I'm glad that you and your wife are able to take to the kind of life you prefer. After all, that's the most important thing. But I'll be sorry to lose you.'

'There you are!' said Dab-Dab to Jip as soon as the man had left the wagon. 'Another getting rich and retiring from the Dolittle Circus. While the Doctor goes on slaving without a penny to his name! Dear old Puddleby, will we ever see it again! I often wonder! All the Doctor ever saves up is new responsibilities and cares — like this young red-headed nuisance.'

With the departure of the menagerie keeper the duties of Manager Dolittle and Matthew Mugg were increased. For until a new man was found to fill the post they had to take turns looking after the animals. And this was not made easier by the young adventurer, who insisted that he take the keeper's place and could hardly be kept out of the menagerie at any time.

But the next morning, to Dab-Dab's great delight, the youngster's mother at last turned up. When she demanded her child the Doctor took her over to the menagerie and, expecting her to be most delighted to find her boy safe, showed her the lad sleeping peacefully between the weary-eyed elephant's knees. With a shriek she clutched the child to her bosom and turned upon the poor Doctor in a fury.

'How dare you keep my son with your wild animals?' she screamed.

'But that was what he insisted on himself,' said the Doctor. 'I didn't want him to sleep here — neither did the elephant.'

'I never heard of such heartless cruelty,' yelled the woman. 'I'm going straight to the police station this minute. I'll have the law on you for this, you — you monster!'

In a storm of tears — in which the red-haired one joined — the woman departed — and did actually go and report the

Doctor to the police. But, as it happened to be the same station which had harboured the young man for a night, the Superintendent decided that the Doctor was more to be pitied than prosecuted and gave thanks that the young man was at last restored to the bosom of his family.

THE DOLITTLE BOOKS

THE STORY OF DR DOLITTLE. 'A work of genius. It is the first real children's classic since *Alice*.' *Hugh Walpole*

THE VOYAGES OF DR DOLITTLE. 'Children will delight in this book. *Dr Dolittle* wins all hearts.' *The Times Literary Supplement*.

DR DOLITTLE'S POST OFFICE. 'Incomparably the best new book for children of the year.' *Spectator*

DR DOLITTLE'S CIRCUS. 'The purest delight . . . as good as the rest of the books dealing with that immortal and delightful person.' *Observer*

DR DOLITTLE'S ZOO. 'It is with genuine regret that we once more say good-bye to the little man who manages to combine Franciscan heroism and charm with homely sanity.' *Nation*

DR DOLITTLE'S CARAVAN. 'A lively and ingenious "Dolittle", and although at the end of the book he has retired to Puddleby, we cannot believe that he is anywhere near the end of his activities.' *The Times Literary Supplement*

DR DOLITTLE'S GARDEN. 'No books of our time can compare with these for communicating to youthful readers those constant glows of appreciation that make them gurgle with joy.' *Daily Telegraph*

DR DOLITTLE IN THE MOON. 'Each generation cries for the moon in turn, and the very newest one will find in these pages not something to cry for, but something to completely satisfy their fleeting fancy.' *Spectator*

DR DOLITTLE'S RETURN. 'It is, indeed, good news that this most lovable man has returned from the moon.' *Lady Cynthia Asquith* in the *Daily Telegraph*.

DR DOLITTLE AND THE SECRET LAKE. 'Humorous, eventful, and never condescending in tone.' *Irish Times*

DR DOLITTLE AND THE GREEN CANARY. 'Dr Dolittle long ago joined the small band of those chosen by children as worthy of more than casual notice.' *Manchester Guardian*

DR DOLITTLE'S PUDDLEBY ADVENTURES. 'Hugh Lofting will take his place among the immortal humorists who have given pleasure to countless millions of readers.' *Children's Newspaper*

JONATHAN CAPE
THIRTY BEDFORD SQUARE, LONDON

All now available in Puffins

ANIMAL STORIES

Ruth Manning-Sanders

Here is a delightful collection of seventeen true stories about all sorts of unforgettable animal characters. They range from a humble hedgehog and a wounded seagull, to the more awesome lion and gorilla and elephants. It's impossible to pick a favourite – horse-lovers may vote for Billy the 'Little Military Learned Horse' that laid the table, others will prefer Shep the collie who really did understand every word his master said, or even the author's own pet, wicked Jacka the crow.

THE BONGLEWEED

Helen Cresswell

Becky's father was head man at Pew Gardens and had always taken his work as seriously as a religion. To Becky it seemed rather silly to keep crossing one plant with another, so she wasn't particularly impressed when her father planted some unknown seeds in the tropical house on Monday and she found that by Wednesday they were two feet high. She christened them Bongleweed, thinking they were just a joke – until the ones she planted herself grew three feet in one night! And when they began clambering and creeping over the wall, people began to be frightened.

THE OWL HOOTS TWICE AT
CATFISH BEND

Ben Lucien Burman

It was a wonderful day in June, and Doc Raccoon and the other animals of Catfish Bend were peacefully enjoying themselves. Suddenly there was a crashing in the brush, and a big grey fox came rushing out. 'Save me!' he panted. 'I've run away from the Zoo in New Orleans. The keepers chased me up the river, but I threw 'em off the trail. I hope you'll let me stay at Catfish Bend.'

For a few weeks all went well, but terrible trouble was coming. For the grey fox wanted to run Catfish Bend for himself, and to break down the honourable pact between the birds and animals which had made this such a happy place.

For readers over eight.

A NECKLACE OF RAINDROPS

Joan Aiken

'Well!' said Aunt Lou. 'I thought of living in plenty of places, but I never thought of living up in the sky! What shall we find to eat up here?'

'That's easy,' Emma said, and it *was* easy too. The fact is that many impossible things seem easy with an imagination and a storytelling power like Joan Aiken's. And never more so than in this collection of beautiful, scintillating, magical, poetical dreams and fancies which are very like the necklace of raindrops in the title story.

Heard about the Puffin Club?

. . . it's a way of finding out more about Puffin books and authors, of winning prizes (in competitions), sharing jokes, a secret code, and perhaps seeing your name in print. When you join you get a copy of our magazine, *Puffin Post*, sent to you four times a year, a badge and a membership book.

For details of subscription and an application form, send a stamped addressed envelope to:

The Puffin Club Dept A
Penguin Books Limited
Bath Road
Harmondsworth
Middlesex UB7 0DA

and if you live in Australia, please write to:

The Australian Puffin Club
Penguin Books Australia Limited
P.O. 257
Ringwood
Victoria 3134